"I love y.... ...., ..., ..., ...
asked.

She was elated, her heart filled with joy. This was
what Cynthia needed to hear. She nodded and answered, "Me too."

"Good, because you are my life. I don't think
there ever was or will be anyone else for me. Sometimes I make mistakes, but everything I do is for us,
for the life we deserve. You're part of me, always remember that."

Cynthia stroked David's cheek, feeling a sensuous current pass between them. He took her hand,
turned it over, and kissed her palm. Leaning closer,
he touched her lips with his, stirring a gentle fire
within her.

David claimed her lips, deepening the kiss. Her
lips parted willingly and his tongue found hers, savoring her taste as if she were sweet nectar. The kiss
sent her emotions into a wild swirl and her pulse
leaped with excitement.

David parted her robe, feasting his eyes on her
smooth brown flesh. His hands slid inside her robe,
making her tingle at each place that he touched.
His fingers molded her body to the contours of his
hands through the lace of her bra.

He popped the fastener, slid the straps off her
arms, and tossed the garments on the floor. At the
same time, she unbuttoned his shirt, kissing David's
smooth caramel skin. He shuddered with delight,
moaning, "Oh, Cynthia."

Circles of Love

KAREN WHITE-OWENS

ARABESQUE

BET BOOKS™

BET Publications, LLC
http://www.bet.com
http://www.arabesquebooks.com

ARABESQUE BOOKS are published by

BET Publications, LLC
c/o BET BOOKS
One BET Plaza
1900 W Place NE
Washington, DC 20018-1211

All Kensington Titles, Imprints, and Distributed Lines are available at special quantity discounts for bulk purchases for sales promotions, premiums, fund-raising, and educational or institutional use. Special book excerpts or customized printings can also be created to fit specific needs. For details, write or phone the office of the Kensington special sales manager: Kensington Publishing Corp., 850 Third Avenue, New York, NY 10022, attn: Special Sales Department, Phone: 1-800-221-2647.

First Printing: July 2004
10 9 8 7 6 5 4 3 2 1

Printed in the United States of America

*This books is dedicated to my friend
Emita Odom Shuler.
Thank you for your help and support.*

Chapter 1

The patio door slid open, then closed. Cynthia heard the heels of David's shoes clicking against the concrete as he strolled toward her. Without a word, he encircled her waist with his warm arms, molding her against the hard planes of his body. A sensuous fire sparked between them. Cynthia relaxed, sinking into his cushioned embrace, while drinking in his subtle scent, as the smooth silk of his trousers brushed against her bare legs.

Eyes shut, Cynthia smiled, creating a mental image of David. Six feet tall with skin the color of melted caramel and copper eyes that sparkled when he got excited, David presented the picture of a successful businessman. Hair the color of midnight lay in waves around his head.

"Hey, hey, now," David whispered in the deep sensual rumble that always stirred her. "How come you're out here?" He twisted a finger around the tip of her ponytail and tugged gently. "In case you hadn't noticed, the party's inside."

"I know. I wanted your family to have a few minutes of privacy."

Tenderly, he rocked her back and forth. "Why? You're family, too."

Cynthia shrugged, at a loss to express her feelings.

David kissed her cheek. His lips moved along her jawline, stirring a gentle fire. "Come on. What's up?"

In the darkness she arched her neck, offering David free access. He accepted her silent invitation, nibbling on her earlobe. A ripple of excitement made her quiver in response. If he hadn't been holding her, she'd probably sink to the floor.

"Why do you think something's wrong?"

David laughed jovially. "You're too quiet. I haven't heard you say ten words in the last hour, and you *always* have something to tell me. The whole family is celebrating inside and you're out here on the patio." He swiped another kiss and asked, "Do you want me to continue?"

Smiling into the night, Cynthia shook her head, linking her fingers with his. "No, attorney Dave. You know me well."

"Then what's going on in that head of yours?" He nudged her with his hip. "Tell me."

There were many things going on in her head, most of them involving him and their relationship. But one situation needed immediate attention.

Turning her to face him, he cupped her bottom, drawing her against him. She felt the instant leap of his flesh as he stirred and grew hard.

"I've missed you," David whispered, holding her close.

"I feel you. Literally."

He chuckled against her throat.

Okay, that was enough of that. She couldn't afford to be distracted by his charm. After all, the sins of the flesh had gotten her into this mess.

Silence stretched between them like the length of an ocean. Once the words left her mouth, they couldn't be recalled, so she took her time, considering the best approach. In a voice devoid of emotion, she said, "I'm pregnant."

"Are you certain?"

"Yes."

David's hands trailed from her waist, settled over her belly, and stroked the flesh possessively through her shorts. "How far along?"

"Little over a month," she answered in a small voice.

He nodded. "Did you do one of those home pregnancy tests or did you go to the doctor?"

"The home pregnancy test. I have an appointment with the doctor next week."

"Good," David muttered against her cheek. He kissed her and added, "I want to tag along for your appointment. Are you all right? Is the baby okay?"

"I'm fine. The baby and I are doing well. At least as far as I know, we are," she answered in a breathless whisper.

"Good, good." He nodded, drawing in a deep breath and letting it out in tiny increments. "Well."

What did that mean? she wondered, irritated and uncertain of his remark. *Was that well good or well bad?*

Cynthia held her breath, praying he would speak the words she needed to hear to make everything right. *Please, David, don't let me down. I need you. I need you to smooth things over for me.*

"I guess we need to get married."

Disappointed, Cynthia fought back tears. Her lips were pressed shut so no sound would burst out.

As marriage proposals went, this one didn't work. Granted, a baby hadn't been part of their plan, at least not at this juncture. But Cynthia believed David would offer more, want more with her. She didn't expect him to propose on bended knee, but she had hoped for a declaration of love, possibly some enthusiasm at the prospect of becoming a father.

This practical attitude toward their spending the rest of their lives together bugged her. He spoke as if they were planning a weekend getaway. Actually, he'd displayed more enthusiasm when they'd planned their last vacation. Cynthia didn't want David to feel as if he had to marry her. She wanted him to marry her because he loved her and wanted to spend the rest of his life with her and their baby.

"Cyn? Did you hear me?"

"Yes," she answered, careful to maintain a neutral tone.

"What do you think? We can go to Vegas and do the do." David pulled her more snugly against him, warming to the topic. "In and out. I wouldn't have to take a day off. That's good for me. If we do it over a weekend, maybe the family can join us and we can make it a big party."

"I don't know." She searched for a way to explain her fears, her desires, her needs. David should understand her. How could she have spent so many years with him and yet he remained so clueless?

"Your place has one bedroom, right?"

She nodded.

"Mine's bigger. Three bedrooms, plus my office. Once we get married, we can close up your apartment and you can move in with me. We'll have to get you out of the lease. That shouldn't be a problem, though. I'm an attorney, you know," he teased, kissing her cheek. "You've got your keys. Come on over and start decorating whenever the mood hits you."

Cynthia listened as the bottom fell away from her dreams. Decorating the nursery alone didn't appeal to her. In her dreams, David played a major part in every aspect of her pregnancy.

David continued, talking more to himself than to her. "Wow! A baby. Our baby."

She wanted a home, a house that belonged to them in a safe, secure neighborhood, away from the rush-hour traffic and pricey high-rise apartments. They needed a place where they could raise their family together. "Have you thought about buying a house?" Cynthia asked.

David turned her and gazed into her face as if he could read her expression in the dark. "Why would I do that?"

"If we have more kids, we'll need a bigger place. Plus, at the end of the day, don't you want to physically get away from the area where you work? I mean, don't you have a hankering for a place of our own? Our private castle away from the rest of the world?"

"No," he vetoed. "I like downtown. Look at the flip side of things. The apartment is conveniently located in the center of town. I work there and the courts are there, everything is where I need it. Besides, I like the lifestyle. Just because we're going to have a baby doesn't mean we have to completely change our lives. I'm not ready to give up my place for a house in the burbs. Maybe later, but not now. I don't see myself mowing the lawn or shoveling snow."

She sensed that she had already lost this battle, but something within her felt compelled to continue the fight. "I just think we'd do better if we bought a home now. Let's be honest. Nothing gets cheaper, just more expensive."

"Nah." David wrapped his arms more securely around her. "Let's stick with my place for now. Remember, this pregnancy is a surprise. We don't want to make too many changes. The baby is the biggest change I'm ready to deal with."

Cynthia shut her mouth. David had stopped her with his comment about the baby. She hoped he didn't believe she tricked him into marriage with a planned "accidental" pregnancy.

"I didn't do this deliberately. David, you do believe me?"

"I know. We were both there. Obviously, our method of birth control didn't work."

Cynthia glanced into his face, trying to see inside his head and heart. "You know, I'm not quite ready to be a mother."

"But it happened, so we have to step up."

"That's for sure."

"Let me see." David nuzzled her neck. "If I count, baby Daniels should make its appearance sometime next February?"

"Yes."

"Why don't you go ahead and quit your job and then you can prepare for the baby?"

Cynthia drew away from him. She could barely make out his strong features in the darkness. How could he suggest such a thing? "Quit my job?" she repeated slowly. "No."

With his hands resting on her shoulders, David said, "Consider it. There wouldn't be any worries about babysitters or nannies. No pickup or drop-off dilemmas. And we wouldn't have to think about day care centers or their staff. Our baby would be safer at home with you than with anyone else."

Shaking her head, she said, "No. No. I'm not ready to be at home all day. I'd go crazy."

"Sweetheart, it's the best thing. Trust me on this. I'm sure Matthew will understand." David chuckled. "Good thing he's marrying into the family."

"I-I-I," she stammered. Shock made it almost impossible for her to speak coherently. "David, I want to work. There are months to go before the baby's born. I don't want to quit my job."

"Why? I make more than enough money to take care of us. Stay home. Enjoy your baby."

"It's not about money. My career is important to me. In the same way yours is to you."

"I never said it wasn't. But, it's hardly the same," David said.

He massaged her shoulders as she tried to reason with him. "I've put time and energy into my career just like you did and I don't want to step out of the work force just yet."

"I understand that, but don't you want to be home to experience everything with the baby? To see that first smile, first step, his first words?"

"Don't you?" she shot back, fighting the edge of panic. David truly surprised her. He always appeared so proud of her career accomplishments. "This is your baby, too."

"Yes, it is. But you'll be the primary caregiver. Someone has to bring in the money. And I think I'm that person because I make a hell of a lot more money than you do. Besides, I'm up for partner, which means I'll be pulling in even more."

"I can do both, work and take care of the baby. It might take a tiny bit of maneuvering, but I'm sure I'll manage."

"Cynthia, you just made my point for me. You don't have to maneuver or manipulate things to work it out."

"I've got a pretty good position and I'm working on some projects that I don't want to turn over to anyone else. Matthew's very open. I'm sure if I talk with him, he'll let me reduce my hours, or work from home, or I can go into the office once a week. We'll figure out something."

"It'll be a lot easier if you just stay home for a while. Marriage and a baby are radical changes."

"Yeah, and I'm the one making them."

David sighed. "Sweetheart, listen to me. I'm not saying you should be home forever, just until the baby is older and we've settled in. Besides, my job will be kickin' when I make partner. You'll have to attend a bunch of company events with me. Plus, we're going to have to host a few social functions. Think about it. You'll be involved in too many different projects for you to keep a job, take care of a baby, and do the things I'll need you to do. Trust me on this. I know what's best for us on this particular front."

Quitting her job wasn't part of the deal. She loved working for Matthew. He allowed her such creative freedom. Why should she make this sacrifice when things were so good? She refused to do that.

A sliver of fear shot through her. In less than ten minutes, he had mapped out their future, minus her input. Was this the way he planned to run their marriage?

David appeared quite pleased with himself, now that he'd made all the decisions. Cynthia wasn't happy, but that didn't seem to matter to him. Right now, he was trying to fit her and her baby into his life, instead of creating a new life that would accommodate all of them.

With a heavy heart, Cynthia stood in the circle of his arms, working on a way to open his eyes. To make their relationship and possible marriage work, she needed him to understand how she felt. In the past, David reacted like an unmovable object when she tried to force him to do anything. She'd found it worked best to ease him into a new situation.

Still, he could be loving and gentle. This attitude was a direct result of learning his life was going to change drastically. Once he calmed down and realized they could have it all—their family, each other, and their careers—he'd be fine. He just needed a little time to adjust. The surprise of learning he was going to be a father had made him a control demon, she reasoned.

Cynthia hugged herself. Finally, she would have her own family: a husband and baby to love and care for. But at what cost? Was she willing to give up a career she loved for the mundane existence of wife and mother? *What if he didn't change?* whispered a tiny voice in her head. What if this was how David felt their lives should be? *What are you going to do then?* she asked herself.

Cynthia didn't know. She craved a home of her own and needed her job for validation. Why didn't David seem to understand that?

Holding Cynthia close, David smiled into the darkness. They were going to get married and he was going to be a father. His heart swelled with love for this woman.

Unconsciously, he slid his hand to her belly, stroking the flesh covered by the fabric of her shorts. As he rocked her in his arms, he remembered the first time they met. Cynthia was his sister Lisa's new friend and she had been a hot topic of discussion. Yet, no one in the family had met her. Being concerned parents, David's mother and father had invited Cynthia to dinner and David got his first glimpse of the girl that would eventually become the woman he loved.

Cynthia had blasted through the door, all legs

and mouth. The topic didn't matter, she had an opinion on everything. Within minutes, she held his heart in her hands.

His gaze softened as he took a second look at her. Five feet, six inches tall, with a hearty sprinkle of freckles on her cheeks, Cynthia had shown the promise of being a beauty one day. And that promise had come to fruition.

She wore her auburn hair in a single ponytail that sat on the crown of her head and swung from side to side when she moved. Her clay-brown eyes danced with excitement behind a pair of glasses. She was cute, very cute, David remembered. Her presence had made it difficult for him to maintain his facade of indifference, especially after she became a permanent fixture around the Daniels house.

Raised in the foster care system, she presented a tough exterior that never cried in front of people. However, as she made a place for herself among the Daniels clan, her hard outer shell faded and a caring person shined through.

He couldn't let her know he cared, so he played big brother to both Cynthia and Lisa. But as Cynthia matured, they became closer, less sibling-like. By the time she asked him to be her date for the senior prom, they were a couple.

Returning to the present, David made a silent promise to Cynthia. He would do everything in his power to make her life perfect and give her everything.

Just then, she stirred in his arms.

He kissed her cheek. "It's time to go in. I want

to tell the family our good news. There's no point in waiting." He let out a hearty chuckle. "This has truly been an eventful day. Vee, Lisa, and now us. My parents are going to flip."

Chapter 2

Hands linked and with a heavy heart, Cynthia followed David reluctantly into the house. Unlike David, she didn't feel that they had settled their future. Her thoughts were congested with fear. In her opinion, things were still unresolved and she wished he would keep their business under wraps until they talked some more.

The moment the patio door opened, Mr. Nick spied them. "Hey, you two, what have you been up to?"

As if they'd been caught sneaking in after curfew, they stopped and muttered in unison, "Nothin'." With the whole family's eyes on them, Cynthia shifted a step behind David, using the bulk of his body like a shield.

An expression of understanding as old as time passed over Mr. Nick's face as he nodded and smirked. "Yeah. I bet. You've been on the patio being romantic."

Everyone laughed and cheered.

David cleared his throat and rubbed the pads of his fingers together. "Actually, we have some news."

He glanced around the room at his family, making eye contact with each one.

Silence loomed over the group like a heavy mist. *He's going to tell them,* she thought, as a cold knot stuck in her throat. *I'm not ready.*

Ms. Helen scooted to the edge of her chair. Her forehead crinkled as she studied Cynthia, then zeroed in on David. Mr. Nick folded his arms across his chest, waiting.

David's arm snaked around Cynthia's shoulder and sealed her against his side. His hand slipped up and down her arm, warm and assuring, in a possessive gesture. "It's been an event-packed afternoon, but I've got one more . . . no, two more things to add to the day. First, Cyn and I are getting married."

Lisa gasped, rushed to Cynthia, and hugged her. Joy bubbled in her laugh and shone in her eyes. "I'm so happy for you. Maybe we can do the double wedding thing." She turned to Matthew. "What do you think? Do you mind sharing that day with another couple?"

All eyes were on Matthew, yet he appeared self-assured and content. Amusement flickered in the depths of his multicolored gaze. He stretched his arms across the back of the sofa. "Whatever you want and makes you happy. I'm with you."

The rest of the family offered hugs and kisses along with their congratulations and well-wishes.

Mr. Nick lifted the milk jug. "This one's almost empty. I'm going downstairs and bring up another. See, Helen? I told you I needed to start earlier this year. There's been a lot of celebrating today. Looks like we've got more to come."

"Hey, Dad. Don't leave just yet." David placed a restraining hand on Mr. Nick's arm. "There's an additional something—something Cyn and I need to tell the family before we start celebrating."

Mr. Nick's bushy brows lifted. "Really?"

"Along with getting married, we're expecting a baby. You and Ma are going to be grandparents twice next year."

"I knew it! I knew it!" Ms. Helen jumped to her feet and wrapped an arm around Cynthia, then David. "There was something different about you today. Something had to be going on. Congratulations." She took Cynthia's face between her hands and tenderly kissed her cheek. "Nick, we have four daughters now. You've always been one of my children," she said to Cynthia. "Do you think you can start calling me Ma now?"

"Oh, Ms. Helen. I mean M-M-Ma. I'll try." It felt funny and it didn't roll off her tongue very easily. Cynthia wasn't sure she'd be able to do that just yet. She felt far from ready to make that type of change in her relationship with Ms. Helen.

David's hand caressed the length of her arm. His mouth curved into a smile. "You've been family all along. Now we're going to add Daniels to your name. Oh, by the way, Cyn and I are thinking of doing the Vegas thing and hopefully you guys can come along and celebrate with us."

Cynthia's gaze swept David's family but settled on Lisa. Pain, envy, maybe a touch of jealousy etched themselves into Lisa's face before she rearranged her expression. She moved away, giving others a chance to congratulate the pair. Cynthia's heart grew heavy as she watched Lisa move across the room to Matthew. Her withdrawal made Cynthia feel cold and alone.

That thought tore at her insides. Where had her best friend gone? She made a mental note to talk to Lisa as soon as they could get together, away from the family and their men. Lisa was hurting and fighting hard to hide it.

Cynthia felt momentary panic as her mind jumped on the thought of losing her best friend through life's changes. Especially not now when things were so fuzzy between her and David. Cynthia needed Lisa's clear, concise thoughts to help her work through her issues with her husband-to-be.

Icy fear twisted around her heart when Cynthia remembered how Lisa had reacted to Jenn's pregnancy. Lisa had been lost and hurt, angry that this precious part of life had been denied her. That she could still be disappointed because she couldn't have children was understandable. It took a while for Lisa to put aside her unhappiness and rejoice in Jenn and Eddie's good fortune. It had taken Cynthia weeks to convince Lisa to attend any family functions.

"When?" Jenn rose from the sofa and stopped in front of the couple.

"We haven't settled on a date yet." David glanced around the room at the members of his family. "But I want as many of you as possible to join us."

"I wouldn't mind a trip to Vegas before the baby

comes. What's your plan?" Jenn moved closer to them.

"I thought we might do it on a weekend. Shoot out on a Friday after work and return home on Sunday afternoon. Give you folks time to recoup for work on Monday." David smiled, giving Jenn an affectionate pinch on the cheek. "That way you can't lose all of Eddie's money at the blackjack table."

"Wrong. I don't gamble."

"Sure you do. You're doing it right now. There's a fifty-fifty chance that you'll have a boy or a girl." He pointed at her stomach. "Gambling."

Jenn waved his hand away. "Oh, you." She touched Cynthia's hand. "It's going to be great, two new members of the family. We can help each other out with babysitting and stuff. How far along are you?"

"Six weeks."

She counted on her fingers. "That means you'll have your baby sometime in February. Good. Eddie Junior will be among us and I'll be able to help you, after you deliver and get home from the hospital."

"Thanks, Jenn. I'll probably need lots of help."

"No problem, we're family. That's what we do."

If she married David, this family would become hers and she liked the idea of finally belonging among them. But there were still bigger problems that she and David needed to address.

"Wait a minute. Eddie Junior?" Cynthia said.

Jenn shrugged, grinning a little sheepishly. "I think it's a boy. But we don't know for sure."

"Hey, brother man." J.D. slapped his hand into

David's palm. They shook hands for a few seconds before J.D. pulled him into a bear hug. "Good luck, man. Good luck. I wish you and Cyn much happiness."

"Thanks, little bro, thanks. We appreciate it. Maybe you need to find a good woman and think about settling down."

J.D. laughed heartily and winked at David. "I'll leave that to you."

David reached for Cynthia and drew her close to him.

From the moment Cynthia and David made their announcement about the baby, Matthew sensed a change in Lisa. The subtle but undeniable shift in her mood disturbed him. Stroking his chin, he considered the woman who made his life complete. He wondered what he could do to help her over what might be an emotional trial.

"Lee?" he whispered, moving around the cocktail table to sit next to her.

She turned to him, a faraway expression in her eyes. "Huh?"

"You okay?" Matthew asked, caressing her soft cheek.

"Yeah. Fine." She gave him a pitiful excuse for a smile before concealing her face. "Why do you ask?"

"You got quiet. I just wanted to make sure you're still with me."

"I'm here," she answered in a quiet voice.

At least physically you are, Matthew thought. *But what are you thinking?*

Matthew shuddered as a wave of apprehension assaulted him. They had traveled a rocky road to get to this point. A road paved with Stephen's lies and arrest, culminating in the discovery of Lisa's infertility issues.

Numerous tests and doctors' appointments had netted a minuscule glimmer of hope. Enough hope to persuade Lisa to marry him. It had taken a great deal of persuasion to get a ring on her finger and squeeze a yes from her. Now Cynthia's pregnancy threatened to destroy all of his hard work. Taking Lisa's hand, he drew her to her feet. "Let's get some air."

Without a word, she followed him to the patio door and they slipped outside unnoticed. The instant he had her alone, Matthew wrapped his arms around her and drew her against his body, warming her cool flesh with his own. He tasted her lips, slipping the tip of his tongue inside her mouth, hoping for some encouragement. None came.

Pulling away, he asked, "What do you think?"

"About what?" Lisa answered in that same dead voice she'd used earlier.

"Cynthia and the baby? Are you okay with that?"

Lisa stiffened in his arms. He massaged her shoulders, working to loosen her up. With deliberate casualness she relaxed. "Of course."

He ignored the hurt manifesting in his heart. "Lee?" Matthew rocked her back and forth, but he couldn't stop himself from saying, "Come on. Be honest with me. I want to help."

"I am being honest. I don't need any help. Cynthia and David deserve some good luck and I wish them every happiness."

"You're telling me that Cynthia having a baby doesn't bother you while we may never have any children of our own?"

"I don't want to talk about this anymore." She turned to the patio door. "Maybe we should go back in."

He grabbed her arm, stalling her. "No. This is important. Don't hide your feelings from me. These are the times I want you to turn to me. Lean on me. Let me be your strength." He knew he sounded corny, but he couldn't help it. He was so worried that Lisa would shut down completely. "Please, babe, tell me what's going on with you. Turn to me. Let me know what's going on and how you feel. Tell me what I can do to help you."

"There's nothing going on." She shook off his hand and turned to the patio door. "If you're done, let's go back inside and get on with the party."

"Just a minute," he said. "I'm not trying to push you into anything you don't want to do. But I want you to know that I'm available whenever you need me. All you have to do is talk to me. I'll do my best to come through."

"I told you, I'm fine. Now let's go in."

Matthew took a step away from her. "Okay. Remember, I love you and I'm here when you need me. I'm here."

Chapter 3

Showered and wrapped in David's navy terry cloth robe, Cynthia snuggled into his smooth, emerald leather sofa. She admired the moonlight sparkling like a shimmering silver dollar through the floor-to-ceiling balcony window. Nelson Rangell's sax oozed from the surround-sound system as muted images flashed across the big-screen television.

Cynthia wiggled her toes into the carpet as the tension and stress of the day eased away. She leaned her head against the back of the sofa and sighed. Now that they were alone, she hoped to talk to David about all the plans he'd made earlier this evening. Possibly, revisit some of his ideas regarding what should happen once they married.

David sank into the spot next to her, kicked off his shoes, and stretched. Cynthia couldn't help smiling as she studied the taut muscles rippling under his gray linen shirt. Her fingers flexed, aching to stroke his skin.

"It feels good to get off my feet and kick back," Cynthia admitted, curling her toes into the deep mushroom-colored carpet. "I'm happy for Vee and especially Lisa."

"If anyone deserves to be happy, it's Lisa. Little Bit has suffered through a lot this year. That fool Stephen and the baby stuff. Do you think she's okay with our announcement? You know, our baby?" Worry lines wrinkled David's brow and his voice turned rough. "I don't want her to be upset or hurt by anything that happens between us."

"To be perfectly honest, I'm a little worried." Cynthia adjusted her glasses on her nose. "She got real quiet when we started talking about babies. Plus, she seemed to withdraw, even from Matthew. I hope she'll be all right."

"I noticed." He stretched his arms across the back of the sofa, brushing a damp lock of hair away from her shoulder.

"I'll put some time in with her. See how she really feels about the baby. Maybe I'll pass along a heads-up to Matthew so that he can look out for her."

"That makes sense. From what I've seen so far, Matthew seemed real attentive. He'll help." David squeezed her hand. "Thanks, Cyn. I don't want Lisa to feel left out."

Cynthia ran her hands through her towel-dried hair and sighed heavily. "Me either. I love her dearly." She shut her eyes, breathing deeply. "Whoa, this day wore me out. Vee's party and Lisa's engagement, a lot happened today. I'm tired."

"You're pregnant, you know. That'll wear you out faster than anything." David winked at her. A flash of humor replaced all of his previous worry.

In a mock show of surprise she brought a hand

to her lips and uttered in a fake shocked tone, "Oh no! When did that happen?"

"Cute." David lifted her feet from the floor and stretched her legs across his lap. His long, tapered fingers massaged her calves, easing away the remaining tension.

Cynthia gave him a big cheesy grin. "That's me, cute."

As he reached across the coffee table for a white box, his face turned somber. "You didn't mention us. Aren't you glad? I mean, we're having a baby, plus we're getting married. That's exciting news, right?"

"Yeah, it is." She accepted the Styrofoam container and the clear plastic fork he extended to her. Opening the white box, she sniffed appreciatively. She loved cheesecake and eating it was rapidly becoming her favorite pastime.

His eyes brightened with amusement as he watched Cynthia devour the fresh strawberry swirl dessert from the Cheesecake Factory. "Is this going to be the craving that sends me out of my warm bed in the middle of the night?"

"Oh yeah." Cynthia bit into the sweetest strawberry. She shut her eyes and sighed. "I've gone to the Cheesecake Factory three times this week. The staff is beginning to recognize my face. The way I feel right now, I could practically inhale two or three more slices."

"Whoa, I'm not sure I'll be able to afford you." David shook his head as if he were genuinely concerned, but a sparkle of humor lurked below the surface.

"You never could."

"Really? We'll see about that. Now that I'm on the short list to make partner that's gonna change. I can afford what I want. And that includes you."

"When will you know?"

"Before the end of the summer the senior partners will make an announcement." He leaned closer and said, "Let me have a taste."

"No." They'd played this game many times. Cynthia loved teasing David.

His words carried a heavy edge of playful reproach. "What do you mean, no?"

"I'm looking out for you. I don't want you to lose your manly figure." She caressed his chest through his shirt, fighting the urge to laugh.

"Worry about your own figure. You're the one going to gain weight. Now give me some of that cheesecake." David grabbed at the Styrofoam container, but Cynthia dodged his hands. In a second attempt to reach the white box, he lurched, but failed to reach it. "You little turkey. I can't believe you'd eat that in front of me without offering me a taste."

She shrugged, then playfully warned, "Get used to it. I can promise you that for the next seven to eight months your tasting privileges are canceled. If you want cheesecake, stock up on your own."

"Let me get this straight. You're telling me that although I went out and got you this treat, you don't plan on sharing."

"Correct. I always knew you were smart, attorney Dave. Besides, I should have gone home. There's a whole one in my fridge."

"You turkey."

"You said that already." Cynthia scooped the final morsel onto her fork and waved it just out of his reach. "Want some?"

David leaned close, ready to take the morsel into his mouth. At the last moment, Cynthia snatched the fork away and ate the cheesecake.

He rubbed the pads of his fingers together. The teasing laughter shimmered in his eyes. "Woman, you're going to get it now." His hands moved up her legs and settled at the backs of her knees, tickling her soft, warm flesh. David's hands moved unmercifully up her body until his fingers settled in the curve of her armpits.

The empty box and fork slipped from her hands, sliding to the floor unnoticed. Cynthia couldn't stop laughing. She begged, "Stop! Stop! I can't take it."

"Good. Then you should have thought about that before you ate the last piece."

"Nooo. Nooo," she shrieked, giggling and squirming on the sofa.

"One bite. I don't think that was too much to ask. One bite." He tickled her relentlessly.

"Okay, okay, okay," Cynthia whimpered, laughing so hard her stomach hurt. "Just stop. Look, look." She pointed at the television screen. "Vivica Fox."

David halted and turned to glance at the television. Cynthia shoved with all her might. He landed hard on the floor as she shot off the sofa.

"Sucker."

"Oh, you're going to get it now. I'm on it."

Giggling, she sprinted down the hallway and

made it to David's bedroom, pushing the door shut behind her. He burst into the room seconds later, swung her into his arms, and crossed the room. Laughing and hugging her close, he tumbled with her onto the bed, rolling around on the mushroom-colored comforter.

His warm breath fanned her cheek as he drew her into his arms and looked deeply into her eyes. "I love you. You know that, don't you?"

She was elated, her heart filled with joy. This was what she needed to hear. She nodded and answered, "Me too."

"Good, because you are my life. I don't think there ever was or will be anyone else for me. Sometimes I make mistakes, but everything I do is for us. For the life we deserve. You're part of me, always remember that."

Cynthia stroked David's cheek, feeling a sensuous current pass between them. He took her hand, turned it over, and kissed her palm. Leaning closer, he touched her lips with his, stirring a gentle fire within her.

David claimed her mouth, deepening the kiss. His tongue traced the soft fullness of her lips, seeking entry. Her lips parted willingly and his tongue found hers, savoring her taste as if she were sweet nectar. The kiss sent her emotions into a wild swirl and her pulse leaped with excitement. How she loved the feel of his lips upon hers.

David parted her robe, feasting his eyes on her smooth brown flesh. His hands slid inside her robe, shimmering along her skin, making her tingle at each place that he touched. His fingers molded her body to the contours of his hand, through the lace of her bra.

He popped the fastener, slid the straps off her arms, and tossed the garments on the floor. At the same time, she unbuttoned his shirt, kissing David's smooth caramel skin. He shuddered with delight, moaning, "Oh, Cyn."

Hot, wet kisses nipped at Cynthia's throat, down to her breasts. His tongue caressed her sensitive swollen nipples. Tingling all over, she felt the sensation to the bottoms of her feet. Her hands stroked across his hair-matted chest and circled the rigid nipples.

Kiss after kiss, they grew hotter as they searched for completeness. Almost like magic their clothing fell to the floor and their hot skin met. Reclaiming her lips, David's mouth covered hers hungrily as his hand skipped across her breast, halting long enough to tease her nipple, then moved lower. His fingers played with the enticing indentation of her navel before traveling lower.

David parted the curls protecting her special place and his finger slipped between the folds, caressing the sensitive nub back and forth. Powerless to resist, Cynthia caught the rhythm of his fingers and moaned. A tiny glow began to build inside her and she shifted her hips, following the demands of his hand.

"Come on, sweetheart. Dance with me. Come on, give it to me," he enticed, increasing the tempo of his finger. She danced from exquisite, sensual peak to peak, building to a moment when she felt herself falling headlong over the border. Shimmering on the edge of her climax, David slid into her with one powerful stroke.

Cynthia cried out his name, wrapping her legs around her fiancé's waist and her arms around his neck. She was burning for him. He began to move inside her, so familiar, yet always so exquisitely different. She matched his dance steps, lifting her hips to meet each thrust of his body. Each stroke took him deeper into her warm sheath until she quivered. Lost in the pleasure of the moment, she climaxed. His harsh cry of release followed.

Steam, thick and damp, rose from the bathtub. Fragrant vanilla candles created an intimate atmosphere as Cynthia stepped into a tub of rose-scented water. She sank between David's strong legs and settled her back against his slick chest. As she nuzzled closer, her thoughts returned to his plans for their future.

As far back as Cynthia could remember, she had been in love with David. Being his wife was an honor that she'd always hoped for. But now that the issue had been presented to her, she realized that it wasn't enough. She needed her career, as well as her own life with him and their baby.

Cynthia considered reopening their earlier discussion as she sipped a cold glass of milk. Eyes shut, she stroked the thick, wet hair on his thigh, trying to relax and let the cares of the day ooze from her body. As water lapped over the side of the tub, she switched positions and wrapped her legs around him. His eyelids lifted slowly, revealing deep satisfaction and the remnants of sensual fire.

"Hey," David muttered, encircling her waist with his arms and drawing her against the hard lines of his body. His lips found the soft flesh behind her ear and sucked gently while his hand caressed her breast, rolling the tip between his fingers.

Stay focused, Cynthia chanted silently, shutting her eyes against the enticing sensations. Taking a deep fortifying breath of air, she asked, "Can we talk?"

He groaned and his hand dropped away from her breast and splashed into the water.

"Please. This is important to me," she begged, stroking a damp hand across his cheek. She wanted to make love again, but it was imperative that they resolve this issue. "We need to talk more about your plans for our future and specifically about my career."

David blew out a hot gush of air. "Cyn, do we have to talk about that again? I thought we agreed on everything."

"No. We really didn't," she snipped at him. "You have to understand about my job. I love working for Matthew and it's not fair for you to expect me to leave a place where I'm comfortable and content. There's got to be some way we can compromise on this. If you really believe that I can't work and raise a baby, I need you to explain those reasons to me."

His fingers skimmed along her arm. "This has nothing to do with your abilities. I have no doubt that you can succeed at anything you choose. All I want to do is give you the option to stay home, quit working if you want."

She shook her head. "That's sweet, but that's not the way it came off to me. I felt as if you were dictating my future. That you had taken my choices from me."

He leaned close and kissed her wet shoulder, softening his voice to a husky whisper. "Look, babe, all I'm saying is you don't have to work. You have something a lot of women don't have these days, a chance to stay home and be a full-time homemaker and mother. Enjoy the baby without worrying about a job, bills, and getting up early to drop the kid at day care. Take the break and be there for the baby. What's so bad about that?"

She scrunched up her face, searching for a way to explain. "I appreciate what you want to do. I really do. But I love my job and I think I can do it all, be your wife and a mother, plus continue my career. Do you see anything stopping me?"

"Well, there is the small issue of my making partner. I'll need you for that. Remember, I've mentioned it to you before? The social thing is very important when you're a partner. Dinner parties, company functions, and stuff."

"And couldn't I do *some* of that stuff"—Cynthia used her fingers to create quotation marks—"and work too? It's not like I'm locked into an office every day. Matthew's very flexible with his employees. All I need is a laptop, network connection, and I'm good to go. I can work from home two-thirds of the time and only go into the office once a week or so. The baby can come with me when it's time for parties and stuff. You already have your house-keeper. If time becomes a factor, Sylvia can increase her days."

"I don't know." He ran a hand up and down her arm. "Let me think about it."

"What's there to think about?"

Calm down, Cynthia, she cautioned herself as she remembered what Miss Helen always said, *"You'll get better results with honey than with vinegar."*

"What about your mother? Do you think Miss Helen did a poor job of raising you guys? Did working make a difference?"

"No. Ma was great. I've always admired her for her inner strength. She worked full-time but still found the energy to deal with five kids."

"Good. That's exactly the way I've always pictured your mother. Efficient and well organized. Do you think it's impossible for me to do the same with one baby?"

"Why are you fighting so hard for this job? I know you like it." His hand lifted into the air, then dropped into the water with another loud splash. "We're getting married soon and I don't think it's the best thing for you to continue to work when we'll be trying to settle into our new life. Marriage is a huge change for us. Add a baby, and I believe we've done all that's reasonable for the time being."

Cynthia listened in stunned amazement. Who was this man in David's skin? All his concerns revolved around how she could make things easier for him; to heck with what she needed. This side of David felt wrong and she didn't like it. Before she

uttered the words "I do" they would have to come
to an understanding about their life together and
what he expected from her.

She figured her time would be used more effec-
tively by showing David that she had the skills to do
both—work and care for her new family—rather
than arguing with him. David would see; given
some time, he'd change his tune.

Cynthia opened her mouth to plead her case
once more, but David chose that moment to
change tactics, raining tiny kisses all over her face.
He whispered close to her ear, "Just think about it.
Give it a few days and then if you feel that I'm being
unreasonable, we'll talk about it again. I promise."
He captured her lips in a kiss that made her whim-
per for more.

David wrapped his arms around her, pulling Cynthia closer. Water splashed over the rim of the tub
once more.

He licked the moisture from her neck, working
his way to her earlobe. His hands drifted lower,
fingers slipping easily between the folds of her
heated core and brushing back and forth against
the aching flesh. She gasped, caught in the hot
and cold sensations created by the water and his
fingers.

"David," she panted, fighting to pick up the
threads of their conversation. What had he just
said?

The dirty rat, he knew her all too well. She
couldn't resist him when he teased her this way. She
arched her body against his busy fingers while seeking the hot demand of his tongue. *I'll worry about*

things later, she decided. **This second round of love-making was just what she needed and she didn't plan to miss out.**

Chapter 4

Cynthia stood at the door to the obstetrician's office, wishing David could have been there with her.
They needed to establish a relationship with the
doctor so that the baby and Cynthia received the
proper prenatal care.

Concern furrowed her brows as she studied her
watch. She wanted David with her. Today was a day
they should share. Would he make it to the doctor's
office in time for her appointment? Unfortunately,
a client had called him away, but he'd promised to
meet her as soon as things settled down. That was
than more than an hour ago.

Taking a deep breath, Cynthia opened the door.
Dr. Noah's waiting room was painted in an inviting
rose color. A floral border presented a cheery flair
to the welcoming environment. White and rose
seats lined the wall and a small round table and
chairs were tucked in a corner.

She glanced around the waiting room noting the
half dozen patients, hoping David sat among them.
No such luck.

Cynthia crossed the carpeted floor with renewed
determination and waited at a sliding glass window.

A blonde slid the window open with an inquiring expression. "Good afternoon. May I help you?"

Offering a nervous smile, she played with the zipper on her purse. "Hi, I'm Cynthia Williams and I have a three-thirty appointment with Dr. Noah."

"Welcome, Ms. Williams." The woman smiled and pointed a finger at the green spiral notebook and pen perched on a ledge outside the window. "Sign in. Then we'll get you started on the paperwork. Oh, by the way, I'm April."

Cynthia responded to the warmth in the blonde's smile and voice. "Hi, April, nice to meet you." She glanced around the waiting room. "Did you get a call for me from a David Daniels? He's my fiancé and he's supposed to meet me here."

"Mmm. Let me check." April shifted through a pile of pink messages on her desk and shook her head. "No. I don't see anything."

Disappointed, Cynthia pursed her lips. "Thanks. Now that I think of it, he'll probably catch me on my cell phone. I'll check once I get settled."

"Here you go." April handed her a clipboard filled with forms and offered Cynthia an apologetic smile. "Sorry for so much paperwork, but the insurance companies make us do this. Fill out everything and return it to me. Take your time. Dr. Noah is running a little late, he had to step over to the hospital to deliver a baby."

"Thanks." She took the clipboard and made herself comfortable at the table.

She removed her telephone from her purse, dialed the law firm's central number, and asked for David.

"Good afternoon, this is Autumn Snyder speaking. May I help you?" a woman inquired in a professional tone.

"Oh, I'm sorry," Cynthia said into the phone as her hand drew circles on the clipboard. "The operator must have given me the wrong extension. I'm trying to reach David Daniels's office. Can you transfer me?"

"This is his office. May I help you?"

She must be new to his office, Cynthia thought. "This is Cynthia Williams. Mr. Daniels was supposed to meet me today. I don't want to disturb him if he's in court. Have you heard from him?"

"You are?"

"His fiancée. Cynthia Williams."

"Oh, oh yes. I do remember hearing your name. I'm sorry," Autumn said. "Mr. Daniels was called away to a deposition about an hour ago. We don't know when he'll return."

A twinge of distress coupled with disappointment assaulted Cynthia. David wasn't going to make it.

"Ms. Williams, are you still there?"

"I-I-I," she stammered, finding it difficult to complete a full sentence. "I'm here. Thank you. Will you leave him a message that I called?"

"Yes, certainly. Have a good day." Autumn promptly hung up.

Fighting the urge to cry, Cynthia dug in her purse, found a tissue, and dabbed at her eyes. Embarrassed by her weakness and tears, she glanced around the room hoping the other occupants hadn't noticed anything. *Come on, Cynthia, you're a big girl. You can handle this.*

This wasn't the first disappointment she experienced, nor would it be the last. She had been alone all her life. Today wasn't any different.

Would David always allow his job to preempt their plans? Cynthia wondered. She understood that unavoidable situations would occur, but today was so special, so important to their future and their baby. Plus, this nagging feeling that her needs came second to David's job refused to go away. Brushing her loose hair from her face, she focused on completing the insurance forms.

Twenty minutes later, she gazed at the particularly unsettling papers. Conflicting emotions churned within her when she reached the section about family medical history. The paper rattled in her hands. She'd never had a family, so family history information wasn't an option. She knew her mother's name, Latonya, and that the woman had given Cynthia up for adoption before her first birthday. And only her mother knew anything about her father.

Could her lack of knowledge affect her life and the life of her baby? She felt so helpless. Cancer, heart disease, and diabetes were serious illnesses and she didn't have a clue if there was a history of these diseases in her family.

Preoccupied, Cynthia worked her way through the pile of paperwork in front of her. She didn't notice a thing until she felt warm, male fingers cover her eyes.

"Guess who?" a male voice whispered with laughter.

Eyes shut and a big grin on her face, Cynthia replied, "I'm not sure. Give me a hint."

He tipped her chin up with a single finger, then covered her lips, kissing her softly.

"I know you," she cried, opening her eyes, and her heart lunged madly. "David, you made it."

"I promised you I would be here." Smiling, David slipped into the empty chair next to her and turned the clipboard to face him. "Paperwork and insurance forms, correct?"

Cynthia returned to her work, running her fingers through her hair. "Correct. Did you get everything settled at work?"

"Yeah, for now." He sighed heavily. His hand stroked her neck. "I feel like a doctor on call twenty-four, seven. I don't know what's going on at the office but things have been busier than ever before."

Cynthia caressed his cheek, muttering softly, "Poor Boo-Boo."

He did look tired and that worried her. No one could continue at this breakneck pace without eventually having a meltdown. "Remember, the more cases you win, the more valuable you become to Ruffino, Hartman and Black, and the more they rely on you and your skills. Maybe it's time to ask for additional staff, or a raise, or both. The company will have to evaluate how much they're asking you to do."

"I'm working on the money part. But in the meantime, I hired a law clerk about a month ago. When she's fully trained, I think she'll be a good asset." David lifted Cynthia's hand from the table and looked around the waiting room before kissing her palm. "You haven't seen the doctor yet, have you?"

"No." She tapped the clipboard with her pen. "I've got to finish this first, then I'll be ready to see the doctor."

"Good." He loosened his red silk tie, unbuttoned the top of his white linen shirt, and relaxed more comfortably in his chair.

David's cell phone rang, cutting through the quiet of the room. Cursing softly under his breath, he answered, "Hello?"

Cynthia took her glasses from her purse and perched them on her nose, watching her fiancé closely. He shut his eyes and his lips puckered with annoyance. She listened to whoever was on the opposite end of the call.

"What? When? No. I'm busy," he answered in a coolly disapproving tone. "Do this, get in touch with Prescall and ask him to stand in for me. He's been involved in this case from the beginning and Judge Reynolds will remember him. Call me back once you've squared everything with him."

Her heart hammered in her ears as she listened to the one-sided conversation. This couldn't be happening. If the firm was going to interfere in each family event they shared, what kind of quality of life could they look forward to?

David disconnected the call and slipped the phone inside his gray jacket pocket. With an apologetic expression on his face and remorse in his voice, he explained, "The Clemmons jury came in."

"Attorney Dave!" Cynthia warned from between

clenched teeth. Remembering the last time he had disappointment her this way, Cynthia felt empty and drained. "This isn't fair. You promised. I'm having my first doctor's visit. You should be here with me."

"I know. I'm sorry, sweetheart," he soothed, placing a hand on his chest. "This is not my fault. I had no idea when the jury would come in with a verdict. Don't get upset yet. If Prescall comes to our rescue, everything will be fine. Relax, finish your paperwork, and we'll wait for my secretary to call back." He tapped the clipboard. "There's no need to panic until we've exhausted all of my options."

You would think he owned the law firm instead of working for it, Cynthia thought. "Okay. I'll wait," she conceded, drawing in a deep calming breath of air. "I understand that this isn't your fault. But I'm not pleased."

Crossing the room, she handed the paperwork to the receptionist and then took her place next to David again. He linked their fingers as they waited quietly. She leaned her head against his shoulder and shut her eyes.

David fished his phone from his jacket on the first ring. "Hello? Good. I was waiting. Everything settled?"

Heart pounding, Cynthia sat perfectly still. She seethed with anger and humiliation as she listened.

Agitated, he checked his watch. "Come on, there's got to be someone in the office. Did you try Harris?" He shook his head, massaging his temple with two fingers. "Webster? Jordan? Davison?" Sighing in defeat, he asked, "What time are we

supposed to be back in court? Okay, I'll be there."
Ending the call, he turned to her. "Cynthia?" he
begged, a pleading glint in his eyes.

"No!" she answered angrily, turning away.

His fingers clamped gently over her trembling
chin, forcing her to look at him. "I don't have a
choice. You heard the conversation. I tried to get
someone from the office to stand in for me. I'm
sorry. There's no one available."

"David, this is not the way I want to live. If you
have to jump at every situation, where does that
leave me and the baby? What kind of life will that
give us? You need to think about that." She swallowed hard, trying to control her anger.

"I've got to go," David said, meekly, pocketing
the phone.

"David!" Fury almost choked her and she glared
at him with burning, reproachful eyes.

His eyes clouded over as he weighed the situation. He dropped to his knees in front of her and
cupped her cheek. He didn't care that everyone
in the waiting room was watching. "Please, sweetheart, try to understand. I'll make it up to you. I
will. I really will."

Crossing her arms, Cynthia turned away from
him. "Go if you have to, because I can't talk to you
right now. I'm too upset. This isn't fair."

He stood, leaned down, and tried to kiss her.
Cynthia shifted away from him and his lips grazed
her cheek. "When I'm done, I'll come by your
place and we'll talk. I promise that I'll make this
right for you."

That said, he shoved a hand in his pocket and moved across the room. Seconds later, he was gone.

Furious, Cynthia jerked her phone from her purse. Checking the time, she punched in Lisa's work number, hoping to catch her. Whenever Cynthia and David had problems, Lisa offered calming words of wisdom. Today was a day that Cynthia needed her help.

The phone was answered on the second ring. "You've reached Games People Play and the office of Lisa Daniels."

Cynthia didn't wait for the beep as she disconnected the call and returned the phone to her purse. It looked as if she would have to resolve this problem on her own. Lately, each time she called Lisa, she was either busy or not available.

Sitting in the examining room, Cynthia gripped the strap of her purse and waited as Dr. Noah flipped through the chart.

"Ms. Williams, everything looks fine. One thing I always do is to confirm the pregnancy with a blood test. In the meantime, I'm going to prescribe some prenatal vitamins and I want you to pick up a list of foods rich in iron." The mocha-colored African-American male pushed his black-rimmed glasses up his nose.

Those words were reassuring and relief washed over her.

Dr. Noah's bushy brows furrowed over his glasses. "You didn't complete the family history form. It's important to know what problems might occur during your pregnancy. Let's go down the list and see what we can find."

Her stomach clenched in a tight knot. Clearing her throat, she said, "Dr. Noah, I don't know anything about my family."

His forehead crinkled as he raised his gaze from the clipboard and studied her over the top of his glasses. "What do you mean?"

"I've been in the foster care system since I was about six months old. I don't have any information about my parents." Shifting nervously on the examining table, she looked quickly away from his probing gaze.

"Really? Do you know who your parents are?" Seated on a small round stool, he moved closer to the examining table.

"All I know is my mother's name."

Nodding solemnly, he said, "I see. You are aware that genetics and heredity play important roles in mapping out a patient's health care. In some cases we can even repair and correct problems in the womb before the baby is born. Also, we need to think about you and your health risks." He patted her hand reassuringly. "I don't mean to alarm you. Let me illustrate my point with this scenario. A family history of hypertension could signal a need to treat you as a high-risk pregnancy, to watch your blood pressure, and prescribe medication. That way I'd know I should keep a closer eye on you."

Some of this she already knew, but none of it changed the fact that she didn't have any additional information to offer him. When it came to her parents, she carried a blank slate. "Dr. Noah, I wish I had something to tell you, but, I don't." Cynthia raised her hands, palms up. "Sorry."

"You had foster parents, correct?"

Cynthia nodded.

Dr. Noah eyed her over the top of his glasses again. "Start with them. Find out what they know. Depending on the agency and your parents, sometimes they will leave their medical history so that the child will be aware of possible health risks. That may be the case with you."

She drummed her fingers on her purse, considering his suggestion. "That may not be a bad idea. My foster parents still live here in Chicago. Maybe I'll pay them a visit and see what they know."

He nodded. "Good. That's a place to start."

She hesitated, wondering if she should ask her next question. Dr. Noah had opened the door to this line of inquiries, she figured, so why not? "If that idea falls through, do you have any others?"

"Well, you could try the foster care agency. They have records. They may have paperwork that includes your parents' last known address and you can follow that trail to whatever conclusion you find. Also, you could do a little investigative work and locate them."

"That's a good idea." Find her parents, she liked that. Maybe she could finally have a real family.

"One thing for sure, you're not helpless. There are ways to learn everything you need to know. You might try the Internet. It's a wonderful resource, if you know how to use it properly. If money isn't an issue, you can always hire a private investigator.

They can be expensive, but it depends on what you can afford and how long you plan to search."

She wanted and needed roots and a sense of belonging, and finding her mother could be the key. A warm sensation surged through her like a litany. *Find my parents, meet my mother,* sang in her head. She could learn what happened to make her mother give her up. The bonus was that her child would have a maternal grandmother as well as a paternal one. Maybe then she'd finally feel whole, complete, instead of like a lost urchin that everyone felt sympathy for.

"We have to talk about the downside. Things may not turn out the way you want. You need to be prepared for that," Dr. Noah warned, closing her chart.

"What do you mean?"

He fidgeted with the pen and continued. "If you find your parents, don't expect too much. They may be a disappointment to you, or they may want to keep your existence a secret from their present life."

Focusing on the glass jar filled with cotton balls, she rejected his theory. "I have no illusions. I mean, my mother left me and as far as I know she's never tried to find me. So it would be foolish for me to expect anything from her," she said. But privately, Cynthia couldn't deny the spark of hope gaining momentum within her.

Opening her chart again, Dr. Noah jotted notes as he spoke. "I want to see you in one month. Take your vitamins and leave the stress to someone else. Understand?"

"Understood."

"Good. Don't upset yourself. You don't want to cause any complications. Whether we have that info or not, my concern is for you and the baby. Don't worry." He patted her shoulder reassuringly.

She smiled. "I won't."

Chapter 5

The doorbell sounded throughout Cynthia's apartment. A grand bouquet of yellow, pink, and white roses obstructed the bearer's features through the peephole. Chuckling, she shook her head. One thing was for sure, David knew what worked on her.

She opened the door but blocked the entrance with her body.

"I come bearing gifts." He shoved the roses in her direction. "I'm sorry, sweetheart. I'm sorry. I wanted to be with you, I really did. My job got in the way. Please forgive me."

She took the roses, inhaled the sweet fragrance, fingering the soft petals of a pink flower.

"Can I come in?"

She tapped a finger against her lips. "Mmm. Let me think about it, attorney Dave. Are you certain you don't have a more pressing engagement? Something to do with your job, perhaps?"

"What could be more pressing than us?"

"You tell me." Cynthia held firm to her position in the doorway. "You left me alone. I had to do everything by myself."

"Sweetheart, it won't happen again. I promise."

She scoffed, holding the bouquet like a shield in front of her. "Famous last words. Right now, I'm not sure your promises are worth the time you take to spit them out."

"Come on." David moved closer. The clean male scent of him wafted under her nose and wrapped around her heart.

"Give me one good reason why I should forgive you."

David's features softened and his voice took on a husky, sensuous tone that made her body quiver in response. "I love you and I want to be with you always."

Cynthia replied, "Is that a fact? That's not enough. I need more convincing."

"There's no one else for me. You've always been the one woman who fills every void in my life." He softly placed a kiss on her cheek.

She rolled her eyes. "I don't know about that. I'd say your job means more to you."

"You're wrong. Nothing is more important than you and our baby."

"Prove it," she challenged, folding her arms across her chest.

Confused, he shook his head. "How?"

"Promise me you'll be at the next doctor's appointment."

"I promise, sweetheart."

He mouthed the right words, but did he really mean them? "David, don't make a promise like this if you don't plan to keep it," she pouted.

"This is as important to me as it is to you. I promise," he stated with determined firmness.

Cynthia examined him with troubled eyes and a heavy heart. David promised with the total belief that he could handle everything. But how long would it be before something else popped up? Still, he was the father of her baby and he deserved a second chance. "Okay. We'll see."

David shoved a cake box under her nose. The fresh aroma of caramel filled her nostrils and made her tummy rumble. "Here's a peace offering. I know it's not strawberry. But I remember a time when it was your favorite."

Cynthia's eyebrows rose suggestively and she stroked a finger across his cheek. "Bribery, attorney Dave? Does the Judicial Review Committee know about this?"

He gave her a big, cheesy grin and waved a hand back and forth between them. "This could be our little secret."

"Maybe." She shrugged, then laughed. "Here I believed you were the essence of a true-blue Boy Scout. You never stop surprising me."

His eyes were warm and pleading. "And I won't ever stop. Am I forgiven?"

Cynthia nodded and opened the door wider. "Although it depends on how well you can kiss my feet."

"I'll kiss any part of you that you want me to. How about a sample?" David took her into his arms. She felt the heat from his tall frame penetrate the fabric of her cotton robe. Tenderly, he kissed her lips as a delicious responsive shudder surged through her.

Wanting more, Cynthia lifted her arms and wrapped them around his neck and let him convince her. She quivered, slowly shutting her eyes as she surrendered to the heat of his kiss.

David drew Cynthia against his side. He shoved the door shut with his foot before tossing his suit jacket over a chair in the living room. They strolled into the kitchen arm in arm. "What did the doctor say?"

"Everything's good, I think," she answered, threading her fingers between his.

"What do you mean, think?"

"They took blood for testing."

"Why?" He smoothed the hair away from her face.

"Dr. Noah said he always confirms a home pregnancy test with blood work."

"Makes sense. Anything else?"

"I've got to add some jumbo vitamins to my diet and Dr. Noah wants me to watch how much cheesecake I eat." She tapped the cheesecake box. "He told me if I keep up at this rate, I'll gain too much weight and it'll be hard to take it off after the baby comes. Not to mention how unhealthy the weight gain can be for the baby and me."

"Sounds right. I can understand that."

"Did you have dinner?" she asked.

He ran his hand up and down her arm. "Yeah, I had a burger at the office. More importantly, what did you eat?"

"Grilled chicken breast, mashed potatoes and gravy, plus green beans."

David opened the refrigerator and placed the cheesecake on the top shelf, then removed a bottle of Coke. He filled a glass with ice and soda. "Good. That sounds healthy. Want anything?"

"Nah." Cynthia opened the cabinet under the sink, found a vase, and filled it with water. "These are beautiful," she said, arranging the roses.

From his vantage point at the sink, David watched her as she fussed over the flowers in a glass vase. After a beat, he took her hand and led her to the living room. "Did the doctor give you a date?" he queried, taking a sip of his soda.

"He was a bit fuzzy on that. But if my calculations are correct we're going to have a Valentine's Day baby. I kinda like the idea." She placed the vase on her coffee table. A smile touched her lips. "The colors are gorgeous. Thank you."

"You're welcome. I'm glad you like them." He set his half-empty glass on the end table and reached for her, guiding her around the coffee table and onto his lap. "We're going to have a Valentine's baby? Do you know what we're having?"

Removing her glasses, she laid them on the table and wrapped her arms around his neck, nibbling on his ear. "David, it's way too early. At the four-month period, Dr. Noah wants to do an ultrasound. He might be able to determine the sex at that point."

He took her face between his hands, brushing her loose locks from her face. "What about you? Are you okay?"

"I'm good."

"Yes, you are." David did a double lift of his eyebrows.

"We're not talking about that." She strummed a finger in his face. Deep within her, she felt a surge of desire take hold.

A devilish light gleamed from his eyes. "Too bad. How about later?"

"Maybe. If you're a good boy."

"Oh, I can be very good."

"I have to agree with that. But I do have some things I need to figure out. And I want to discuss them with you."

Drawing away, he searched her face intently. "What's up?"

"At the doctor's office I had to fill out a zillion forms, of course. One form gave me a moment of pause. It really made me think about the baby and myself."

"Go on," he encouraged, stroking her cheek.

"This form wanted information about all our parents' medical histories. Your family stuff I knew because I've been around since I was a kid. But when it came to my own family, I realized that I don't know jack. Even my father's name is a mystery to me. I mean, I know my mother's name, but that's it."

Sympathy played across David's face. "Where is this leading?"

Cynthia swallowed hard, stirring uneasily on his lap. "We both know there's a black hole in my past. A place where I should have information and I don't."

"And?"

"I want to fill that hole."

"We can get around the family history stuff. Besides, not knowing about them has never bothered you before."

A bit embarrassed, Cynthia muttered, "That's not quite true."

"What do you mean?"

"I've always wanted to know."

"Why didn't you tell me?"

She hunched her shoulders, feeling heat burn her cheeks. Frustrated, she removed her arm from around his neck, stood, and began to pace. "I don't know. It never seemed right to burden you with this."

"Who should you burden, if not me?" he asked.

"I'm sorry. I've always wondered about my mother, I just kept my feelings to myself. But having a baby makes it a bit more urgent to know. There's no medical history for Dr. Noah to work with. If there is some bad stuff in my family, it could change how he handles this pregnancy."

Standing, David stepped in her path, stopping her. "Sweetheart, calm down. You're fine. You're going to work yourself into a tizzy over something you can't do a thing about. Don't go borrowing trouble."

"That's where you're wrong. Dr. Noah suggested that I try to find some info about my mother and father. Well, at the very least, my mother. He gave me some tips on how to locate her, like contacting the foster care agency or talking to my foster parents. They may have info that could help me. There's always the chance that my mother may have left their medical histories for me."

"Why wouldn't the Grants have passed on any info they had before now?"

He'd made a good point. "Maybe for the same reason that you always thought I was okay without parents. Because I never said anything."

David took her hand and led her back to his lap. "Cyn, I don't want you to get your hopes up. I mean, what if the Grants don't know anything or the agency refuses to help you? What are you going to do then? This is a recipe for pain and disappointment. And I don't want that for you."

"I know this could all fall apart and I could hit a dead end, David. I can handle that. What I can't live with is the uncertainty, the *not* knowing. Don't you think it's worth the risk for our baby's sake? Ten years from now, I may need to know if my mother had cancer or diabetes or was an alcoholic. There's so much that's lost to me. I want to learn more about who I am, where I came from." Her voice broke and she turned away, fighting back tears.

"You're Cynthia Williams." Gently turning her to face him, he cupped her cheek with his hand and stroked her flesh with his thumb. "The woman I love. You're giving and true to your friends. Don't forget that."

She blushed, holding his hand against her cheek. "Thank you. Dr. Noah also suggested that if I don't learn anything from the agency, I could try a private investigator."

"Wait a minute. A private investigator? Do you realize how much a PI costs?"

"No."

He sighed. "Hundreds of dollars an hour and that's if you get a good one. And you've got to check them out before you hire them. Some will take your money and string you along. Think this through very carefully. Promise me that you'll talk to me before you make a decision."

"I understand all of that. It's time for me to come clean with you. I don't plan to let this opportunity slip through my fingers. I need to know more about where I come from. And I'm going to."

David placed his hands on her shoulders. "Let me make a couple of suggestions. Try your other options first. Check with the Grants, talk to the foster care agency, then if you come up with nothing, let me know. I'll get one of the PIs from the firm. That way I'll know that you won't get conned. Your interest will be protected. Promise me, okay?"

All she wanted was to find out information about her parents. Learn more about their medical history, so that she could be an informed parent instead of a lost one. Studying David's uncompromising profile, Cynthia realized that she might have to do this search alone. If the situation presented itself, she'd politely decline David's offer of help and find her own PI. She didn't want the firm to be involved in her personal business. But first, she'd do what Dr. Noah and David suggested. Do her own research, then take things from there.

Suddenly the lightbulb switched on in her head as she contemplated her next move. Jacob Summers. He was a PI. Jacob had helped Matthew find out how and why Stephen Brock had stolen software from her employer, Games People Play.

If the time came, she'd talk to Jacob and see if he would pick up her case. With his background and connections, he might be more approachable financially.

David drew her attention back to him with a kiss. "It's time to talk about something else. We've got important business to deal with."

Her face scrunched up. "Like what?"

"How about setting a date to get married? Your lease on this apartment? How soon are you going to start working on the nursery? We need to make plans."

Cynthia stroked his cheek, enjoying the warmth of his skin against her fingertips. "Attorney Dave, do you have a date in mind?"

He hugged her close. "First weekend in August? That'll give the family a chance to arrange their schedules so that they can attend, plus you won't be so large that you can't enjoy the day."

She rolled her eyes and responded, "Gee, thanks." That gave her approximately five weeks to get the information she wanted before her wedding. Tomorrow, she'd get things rolling by contacting her foster parents and the agency. "Okay. If that's what you want."

"This should be what we both want, Cyn. If you have another date or something you want to do differently, now is the time to let me know. I want you to have beautiful memories about our wedding day. A couple of days ago you mentioned that you felt I was making all the decisions. Now I'm asking for your input. What do you want?"

Cynthia sat quietly on his lap, playing with her fingernails. "It's fine," she muttered. "I don't have any objections to Vegas. Whatever works."

David studied her for a beat, then said, "Let's move on. I've got something for you."

That piqued her interest. She sat up straight. "Really? What?"

Grabbing his suit jacket off the chair, he fished inside the pocket and produced a velvet ring box. Cynthia's heart raced as he opened it and an engagement ring with four diamonds set in a band of white gold glittered from a bed of blue velvet.

"Oh," she muttered, reaching for the box. "It's beautiful."

He chuckled. "Finally, I've done something that meets with your approval. Now let's make this official." He bent down on one knee and extended the ring to her. "Cynthia Williams, will you marry me?"

Joy bubbled inside her. David had finally gotten things right and realized what she wanted from him. With a hand to her lips, she nodded.

A flash of humor crossed his face and he teased, "Ah! I didn't hear anything."

"Yes. Yes." She threw her arms around him, planting warm kisses on his face.

"Now we're talking," David stated in a voice filled with satisfaction. "You are the most important thing in my life. I love you and I plan to spend the rest of my life with you and our baby and any more babies that we make along the way." He slipped the ring on her finger and said with a faint tremor in his voice, "This ring binds us together. It represents my commitment to you and our family."

Cynthia gazed into his eyes and stroked his cheek as David leaned close and captured her lips in a kiss filled with love. When he did things like this, she couldn't resist him. Admiring the glittering band on her finger, she asked. "Do you want to wear a ring?"

"Mmm, I haven't thought much about it. Maybe." He brought her hand to his lips and kissed it.

"What kind of band do you like?"

"Surprise me."

She nudged him with her elbow. "Come on. You're the one that has to wear it. It would be nice to have some idea of what you would like."

David hunched his shoulders. "I don't know. Let's talk about something else. We can sort the ring stuff out later." He set her on her feet, rose from the sofa, and took her hand. "Now, I've been a good boy, wouldn't you say?" he asked with a double lift of his eyebrows.

"Pretty good."

A gleam of sensual fire shone from his eyes. "How about sealing things with a little David and Cynthia time?"

"Okay. That's sounds doable."

David slipped his arms under Cynthia's legs and swung her into the circle of his embrace. He stood, capturing her lips for a kiss filled with passion and love as he walked.

She muttered against his lips, "I know this is an

exciting moment, but you're going the wrong way. The bedroom's that way."

"I know. I've got a better idea," he explained between feathery kisses. "We're celebrating. Let's do something a little more creative this time."

"Oh? What you got in mind?" Cynthia asked with a saucy curl of her lips. A spark of anticipation nestled inside her.

She was up for a little experimentation. Stopping in the dining area, he allowed her to slide along the length of his hard, heated body before releasing her. The taut muscles under his shirt were powerful and the long length of his arousal nuzzled against her stomach.

David's large hand took Cynthia's face and held it gently, drawing her close. "I love you," he declared as he stripped away her robe.

"I love you." She ran her hand over his broad chest, returning the favor by removing his silk tie. "So what's the plan? I can tell you this, I'm not making love on my table. I have to eat on that table."

"Eat? Who said anything about eating? At least not food." He nibbled on her neck while his hand crept lower, cupping her bottom, and drawing her closer. "But maybe later?"

"You are so bad."

"Yeah, but you love it." He traced her lips with one finger. His touch sent shivers sizzling through her. God, she loved this man and everything he did to her.

Flashing a persuasive grin in her direction, he walked her backward until her legs hit a chair. "Let's take a ride in the chair."

"My . . . my . . . my," she muttered with an upward lift of her brow and an agreeing smile on her lips. "Aren't we inventive today? And they say the romance dies when you start a family."

"It's never going to end between us," he promised, unbuckling his belt and unzipping his trousers. David stepped out of his pants, removed his shirt, and sank into the chair. His rock-hard arousal saluted her.

"Oh yeah." Cynthia grinned seductively as she stepped between his spread legs and took his face between her hands. She planted soft kisses on his face and along his jawline before she sucked on his ear. "Guess what?"

"What?" he whispered, running a finger along her spine.

"I love you."

"I love you too." His hands spread across her tiny waist and his mouth became reacquainted with her breasts. Moving lower, he nipped at her soft curls with his teeth as he inhaled her womanly fragrance. "You taste so sweet," he told her sensuously.

Moaning, Cynthia nearly collapsed on the spot. Her hands shook as she tried to steady them on his shoulders.

David's hands spread around her waist, positioning her center above him. Then, slowly and with the greatest care, he lowered her until he was sheathed completely by her body.

Cynthia felt him throbbing inside her. She hooked a foot around the front leg of the chair for better leverage and rose slightly, then sat down on his lap. David gasped, gripping her hips. He rocked himself beneath her, withdrawing and thrusting inside her body again and again. Each stroke came stronger and deeper, building until she felt the first flutter of ecstasy.

Surging to his feet with Cynthia in his arms, he lowered her to the floor. Still inside her, he gave her a hard impassioned kiss as he thrust into her body, moving them closer to completeness.

She wrapped her legs around him and trailed her fingers up and down his back. His demanding rhythm wrapped her in overwhelming pleasure; their bodies were in exquisite harmony. Aching with passion, Cynthia sobbed his name, shattering into a million glowing pieces.

Chapter 6

This is the perfect opportunity, Cynthia decided, as she made her way up the Danielses' walkway. She stopped, smoothed the wrinkles from her sleeveless midcalf linen dress, and readjusted the strap on her jade sandals.

Miss Helen had requested that Matthew and Lisa's wedding party meet, and Cynthia felt certain that Jacob, Matthew's good friend, would be there. If things worked out, she hoped to maneuver a private moment with Jacob and ask him for his investigative help.

Pleased with her plan, she did a sassy little dance up the steps. She didn't feel comfortable with David's response to her request to find her mother. Instead of his cheering her on, she felt as if he was trying to discourage her somehow. Finding her parents was far too important and she wasn't going to let anyone or anything stand in her way.

A cold shiver spread over her as she remembered David's warning. He'd been correct about the cost of private investigators. Their fees and daily expenses were well beyond what she could afford if it became a lengthy search. But Jacob might be the person to help her without charging her a fortune or demanding the child she was carrying as payment.

Opening the front door, she followed the chatter and the Temptations' "My Girl" to the family room where the Daniels clan gathered to discuss Lisa and Matthew's wedding. The spicy aroma of jalapeños and ground beef permeated the family room.

Jacob and Matthew stood huddled in the corner near the patio door, talking quietly. She glanced around the room and found Jenn, Eddie, Vee, and J.D. playing cards as they nibbled on a tray of nachos.

Cynthia moved to Matthew's side. "Hey," she greeted, giving his hand a quick squeeze. "Where's Lisa?"

A momentary look of discomfort crossed his face, but he maintained a calm tone. "As far as I know, she planned to drive herself here. She needed to do a couple of things before she arrived." Pointing at the man next to him, Matthew asked, "You remember Jacob Summers, don't you?"

With an outstretched hand, she turned to him. "Yeah, I do. How're you doing?"

Gray snappy eyes looked out from Jacob's sun-toughened face. He smiled at her, taking her hand in a firm grip. "Good. It's nice to see you again."

Matthew slapped his buddy on the back. "Jay's agreed to be my best man. You two will be paired up together for the wedding."

"Oh." *And good*, she thought, feeling hope surge through her. She'd have plenty of time to work with him and see what he could do.

Miss Helen handed Cynthia a glass of punch. "Hi, darlin'. How are you and my baby doing?"

"Fine. Just fine. David called me on my cell phone. He's running a little late, but he promised that he'd be here within the hour, Miss Helen."

She nodded. "That's no problem. Lisa isn't here yet. And I thought I told you to call me Mom. You're part of this family now."

"Sorry, M-M-Mom." Cynthia smiled apologetically.

"Don't worry about it." She patted Cynthia's shoulder. "It'll come in time."

"Helen." Mr. Nick waved her over to the door.

She nodded back at her husband. "Let me see what this man wants. Excuse me." Miss Helen moved away from the small group.

Turning back to Jacob, Cynthia said, "Don't you live in California? Are you planning to stay in Chicago until the wedding or fly back and forth?"

The cell phone in Matthew's pocket rang. He glanced at the illuminated screen. "Excuse me. I need to take this. I'll be back in a minute."

Silently, they watched Matthew leave the room and move into the hall.

"San Diego's home. But I'll be here way past the wedding. There's still stuff I've got to settle connected to Stephen Brock. I'll be here until I've completed the investigation," Jacob explained.

Shaking her head, Cynthia said, "Good old Stephen. He's your man if you want to destroy a company by selling the most profitable software to your competition."

"That's him. He almost took Games People Play

under. Good thing we were able to track his sales on the Internet." Jacob swirled the liquid in his glass. "Why do you want to know how long I'll be in Chicago?"

"I was wondering if—if you're taking on clients." She held her breath, waiting for his answer.

Jacob's blond eyebrows rose. He moved closer, shielding her from the rest of the group. "Intriguing. Tell me more."

"There's a project that needs your expertise," Cynthia said as she sipped her punch.

"What kind of project and what does it entail?"

"You know plenty of ways to track a person, am I correct?"

"Correct."

"That's good."

Scratching the side of his face, Jacob swallowed the contents of his glass. He made his way to the makeshift bar and poured another shot of cognac and returned to her side before asking indulgently, "What do you need from me?"

"How do you know it's for me?"

His mouth twitched with amusement. "It's a fair guess. Tell me how I can help you. Who or what are you trying to find?"

"I need . . ." She paused as the tip of her tongue moistened her upper lip. "Information about my mother."

"Why don't you ask her whatever it is you need to know?"

She shrugged. "Can't. I don't know her. I've been in foster care most of my life."

"I'm sorry."

"It's nothing for you to be sorry about. You didn't know and it's not your fault."

"Let's get back to business. What kind of info?"

"Mostly medical. You know, health issues."

"Mmm-hmm." Jacob studied her as if he could see into her soul. She felt the faintest surge of heat fill her cheeks.

"You don't want to meet them? You just want to have their health history. Correct?"

Until that moment, Cynthia had refused to think past learning more about her parents' medical history. Now that the question had been posed, part of her admitted she wanted to meet her mother, talk to her, learn all the reasons behind why her mother had given her away. And a greater part of her wanted to establish a relationship with the woman who gave her life.

"Could you find her, maybe get an address where I could look her up?" she asked in an eager whisper.

"Whatever you want. I could do it," he offered enticingly. A faint light twinkled in the depths of his gray eyes.

Cynthia's breath caught in her lungs and for a moment she hesitated over her plan. She noticed a spark of something additional, more than curiosity. She shook her head and glanced at Jacob. Friendship was reflected in his eyes.

She drew closer, lowering her voice a fraction. "Okay, here's the big part. How much? I understand from a few of Matthew's comments that you are top of the line."

"Generally, you couldn't afford me," he stated matter-of-factly.

All of her hopes died a sudden, unpleasant death. Putting on a brave face, she said, "Which means how much?"

"Five bills a day, plus expenses."

Five hundred dollars a day! Her heart almost exploded in her chest. Jacob wasn't kidding when he said she couldn't afford him. She'd need three jobs to afford his services. Pride kept her from revealing her true feelings. Smiling through her disappointment, Cynthia said, "Thank you, I appreciate you taking the time to talk to me." She turned away, tears swimming in her eyes. A hand on her shoulder halted her.

"Cynthia, stop. Let's talk some more."

"About what? You're not in my budget. I can't afford you."

"Maybe we can deal."

"I don't have anything you need."

"That's where you're wrong. I need some help of my own. Chicago is a foreign world to me. If you'll work with me to find a decent apartment and furnishings, then I'll help you with your project."

She examined his face, trying to decide what he was thinking. "You're serious?"

"Correct."

"I don't want or need a pity party. I mean, I appreciate the break you're trying to give me. But I don't want to be the charity case of the week."

"You're not. I don't think you could be even if you wanted to. Do we have a deal?" He held out his hand for her to shake.

Placing her hand in his, she felt an electrical jolt. "Yes. I'd be a fool to turn you down."

"Good. Now answer a question for me. That lawyer fiancé of yours has access to PIs, all types of information, and anything else you need. Why aren't you having this conversation with him?"

"This is personal and—and David doesn't really understand my dilemma." She pointed a finger in the direction of the Daniels family. "Look around you. He's always had this. A family that loves and admires him. What's going on with me doesn't have the same importance to him."

"It should."

"Why do you say that?" Cynthia asked.

"Anything related to you should be important to him."

"Thank you." Cynthia licked her dry lips. "I have one additional request."

"Shoot."

She stole an additional glance around the room filled with David's family and lowered her voice another octave. "I'd like to keep this between us. Okay?"

His eyes searched her face, reaching for her thoughts. "It's no problem."

"Thank you."

Without warning, she felt the familiar warmth of David's hands on her shoulders, massaging her taut muscles.

He kissed her cheek. "Hey, sweetheart. How you doin'?"

"I'm good," she said.

David turned his attention to Jacob and studied

the other man for several silent moments, sizing him up. "You're Matthew's friend from college. I'm David Daniels, Lisa's brother and this little lady's fiancé."

"Jacob Summers." He offered his palm and the two men shook hands.

Wrapping an arm around Cynthia's waist, David said, "I need to steal my girl away."

"We're just talking. Steal away." Jacob spun in the opposite direction, finishing his drink.

"That was totally unpleasant. Something is going on with my sister," David said, as they walked hand in hand to Cynthia's midnight-hued Mustang.

"I know. I thought Miss Helen was going to kill her," Cynthia agreed. "It took her two hours to show up for her own wedding planning meeting. And then she refused to decide anything."

"Yeah. I got that." David opened the passenger door and helped Cynthia into the car. "She's losing it again, isn't she?"

"I think so."

He rounded the hood of the car and climbed in. Turning in the bucket seat, he asked, "Did you see the look Lisa gave Matthew when he asked what kept her?"

Cynthia nodded.

"I thought her skull would crack open like they do in some of those horror movies. I was waiting for an alien to pop out and devour us all. She scared the heck out of me." He glanced out the window and turned the key in the ignition.

Cynthia slid a CD into the disc changer as David pulled away from the curb and headed out of the subdivision. Gary Taylor's "So Special" filled the car.

Stopping at the gate to the neighborhood entrance, he checked traffic before making a right turn. "I thought we had resolved all that stuff when Jenn got pregnant. Now we're back to square one."

"David, this is different." He didn't realize how hard everything had hit Lisa. Searching for the correct words, she paused. "I mean, I'm her best friend and it's hard for her to see you and me so happy with the one thing she can't have. She only sees Jenn when the family gets together. Lisa and I work together and we used to talk on the phone all the time or have lunch together. Lisa's scared and she hurting."

"Are you saying she's jealous?"

"No. Not at all. When Lisa says she's happy for us, I believe she means it. But at the same time she can't help being envious of everything we have and what she wants for herself with Matthew."

He nodded. "I can see that."

"Don't think badly of her," Cynthia warned.

"I don't," he assured.

Wetting her dry lips, Cynthia continued, "I know she loves Matthew. But I believe she's afraid to commit to him with this problem between them."

"How do we help her?"

Cynthia shrugged. "I don't know. Maybe we just have to be there for her. Make her understand that we are still her friends and family and that we appreciate what she's going through."

"How do we do that for a woman that won't open up?" David switched on the turn signal before merging into traffic.

"I'm not sure. But I'm going to try dropping by her office and encouraging her to talk."

"That could work." He took his eyes from the road for a moment and pointed in her direction. "I'll leave it to you. Let me know how things turn out and what I can do to help. If things don't shake out well, we'll have to talk to Ma and Dad and see what they say."

"I don't want to worry them if I can keep from it."

"I know what you mean. But they may be the only people who can reach Lisa. We need to keep that option open. Agreed?" David snatched a glance in Cynthia's direction.

"Agreed, attorney Dave. To be perfectly honest, I haven't talked to her since we told everyone that I'm pregnant."

"How can that be? You work at the same company."

"David, we may work in the same building, but Lisa's never in her office or she makes an excuse to cut me short when I telephone her."

"Did you get a look at Matthew?"

Cynthia moaned remorsefully. "Yeah, I did. I feel for the man. You can see that he doesn't know what to do with your sister and she's not making it easy for him."

"No, she's not." David paused to compose his next sentence carefully. "I have a question for you. What's the deal between you and the surfer boy?"

Shocked, Cynthia stared openmouthed at David. Gathering her thoughts, she answered, "His name is Jacob."

"What was going on between you and Jacob?" David uttered his name with all the venom he could muster.

"You know, he's a PI. Jacob helped Matthew get evidence when Stephen was stealing from Games."

"I heard a little about it from Ma." Turning onto the freeway, he sped up to enter traffic.

"I figure he'd know some maneuvers that would help me track down my mother on the Internet."

"Which means what?"

How would she answer that question without lying to him?

"Come on. What's up?" he asked when she didn't respond.

"Jacob gave me some ideas where I should start my search."

Exhaling deeply, David said, "Please don't think I don't care, because I do, Cynthia. But I don't want you to get too involved in searching for your mother. What if you can't find her. Or worse, what if she doesn't live up to your expectations. Please be cautious."

"I am."

"No, you're not. You think finding her will make everything better. I'm not sure that will be the solution."

"Why are you so against me finding her?"

"I'm not," he denied. "My concern is for you and how you will feel if this goes awry. I don't want you to be hurt. Can you fault me for wanting to protect you?"

"I'm a grown woman and I know how to take care of myself. I'm not going to get hurt. The worst that can happen is that I don't find her," she said defensively.

Silently, he drove along the freeway.

Cynthia touched his arm and felt the muscles jerk under her fingertips. "David, I know what I'm doing. Give me a little credit."

"I know you believe you know what you're doing, but I'm worried. If I can't stop you, let me get one of the firm's PIs to work on the case. Don't deal with that surfer boy."

"Don't connect the firm with my business. Jacob gave me some good ideas. Let me try them first." She twisted in the seat, facing him in the darkness of the car. "Okay?"

His expression cleared. "Just be careful. If you need anything, come to me"

"If I can't figure things out, you'll be my first choice for help, attorney Dave."

She didn't want to keep anything from him, but she believed his reluctance to help her find her mother would cause a rift between them. Working with Jacob, she could track her mother and get the information she needed without involving David. *This is the best approach*, she thought. Keep David out of the loop and work with Jacob. When she found her parents, she'd introduce him. Voila!

Chapter 7

Cynthia connected her computer notebook to the LCD projector, picked up the remote, and displayed the first slide from her PowerPoint presentation. The sun's rays faded the picture on the screen. Concerned, she strolled across the royal-blue-carpeted floor and adjusted the oatmeal-colored vertical blinds until the slide sharpened and cleared. Pleased with the results, she returned to her premier slide and turned off the projector.

Her stomach danced a jig and she placed a protective hand over her belly, fighting to control a fit of nerves. This project meant a lot to her. This was her opportunity to give back to the community that helped raise her.

She ducked into the connecting bathroom and checked her appearance. She had chosen her outfit and accessories very carefully this morning. The plum Donna Karan linen pantsuit gave her a sense of power and control. Whenever she needed additional luck, she always wore the pearl earrings that David gave her when she had gone on her initial interview for her job.

Buttoning the thigh-length fitted jacket, Cynthia

studied her reflection in the mirror. Granted, only a few weeks had passed since she discovered that she was pregnant, but she was pleasantly surprised to discover that the suit still fit perfectly. Smoothing her hair into place, she returned to the conference room to wait.

"Hi, Cynthia." Dressed in an army-green light-weight suit and a matching silk shirt, Matthew entered the conference room and waved at her. His green tie had white shells embroidered on it.

She returned his wave. "Hey, Matthew. How are you?"

"I'm good." He strolled across the room to the coffee setup and picked up a mug, filling it with coffee. "I hope you don't mind, I've asked Jacob Summers to sit in on this meeting."

"Fine with me." Cynthia hunched her shoulders. "But I do want to know why"

"As my Internet guru, Jacob has his hands in a lot of pies. He might be able to add to our discussion," Matthew explained, moving back to the walnut conference table with his mug. He checked his watch. "He should be here any minute."

She nodded. The palms of her hands became sweaty and perspiration inched down her neck as she mentally reviewed her presentation. Jacob was top-notch and always on his game; she hoped she'd covered everything.

The man in question entered the room with Lisa in tow. Today, he wore a pair of jeans, an open-neck navy work shirt, and Michael Jordan sneakers. His ruffled blond hair looked as if he'd spent the day running his fingers through it.

Lisa looked coolly professional in a soft pink two-piece dress and matching knee-length jacket. White Diamond perfume trailed her steps as she approached the conference table.

"Thanks for coming, Lisa, Jacob." Cynthia turned to Matthew and said, "A few more members of the team are due any minute and then we'll get started."

Matthew followed Lisa's movement with his eyes, then rose, strolling across the room to touch her arm. "How you doing, Lee?" he asked in a husky whisper.

"Fine," Lisa muttered, backing away from his hand. She continued around the table, slipped into a chair near a coworker, and opened her briefcase. She refused to look in Matthew's direction, concentrating on her materials instead.

Perry Lewis, the director of new products, Kent Lane, the marketing director, and Luther Grant, the director of finance, marched into the room. Luther sat near the head of the table while Perry and Kent grabbed coffee before taking positions around the table. Introductions were made, then Cynthia took a deep breath and brought the meeting to order.

Cynthia tapped the remote and the LCD hummed to life, filling the projector screen with colorful images. She clicked through the first round of slides, using a laser pointer to highlight specific information on the screen. "We've always created game software that related to movies, current historical events, or alien invasions. And we've been highly successful. Although these areas are still very popular and profitable, life changes and we need to stay competitive in today's shifting market while answering the needs of our client base."

She switched to a new series of slides, rubbing her lucky pearl earring between two fingers for silent encouragement. A picture of the White House appeared on the screen.

"Recently, President Bush introduced the No Child Left Behind Initiative, which addresses children's educational needs. I say we pick up the gauntlet and create a new division that focuses on helping children's reading, math, and learning skills."

"Interesting." Matthew tented his hands together, turning to his friend. "Jacob?"

"Cynthia may be on to something." Jacob unwrapped the end of a health bar and bit into it. "It's a nationwide problem."

Luther piped in with a statement. "The economy is tight. It may not be the proper time to create a new division."

"True," Cynthia agreed, moving closer to Luther. "But this is a field that is wide open and we could corner the market on software that specifically addresses the problems facing America's children. We'll get the highest endorsement available. The president of the United States is behind this initiative."

Luther tossed a hand in the air. "I'm looking at things from a financial point of view."

"And you should. Your big three auto companies are always looking for ways to expand and broaden their empires. Why shouldn't Games People Play do the same? This is an area that will make us look good and we're using a client base that we already have."

"These are all good points," Matthew said. "Do you have data to support this kind of shift in business?"

"Yes, we do," Cynthia stated confidently, turning to her friend. "Lisa Daniels has compiled research data, including changes in the market."

Lisa reached into her briefcase and distributed colored folders to the group. "After Cynthia explained this proposal to me, I worked up a prospectus on the project. As you can see, we'd have an initial start-up that would quickly be recovered. These products could be sold to school districts and individuals. With the correct advertising, distribution, and endorsements from some educational leaders this could be huge. We might be able to convince Microsoft to bundle this software into their line. Therefore, every computer that is sold will have our software installed on it. There's a great deal of potential for these products."

Slowly flipping through the folder, Matthew studied the figures. He stroked a finger and thumb across his chin. "Math, science, reading, or learning skills . . . Cynthia, where would you start?"

"I would start with projects that will help reading scores. There is so much additional stimulus to keep children busy," Cynthia explained. "Reading doesn't hold the appeal that computers, computer games, Gameboys, television, videos, and the Internet provide."

"You've got a point there." Jacob rubbed his forehead with a finger. "What type of games would you create? How would they be designed to help students read?"

"When we grew up, board games were our stimuli. Monopoly, Sorry, checkers were the games we played. Studies have shown that there is a direct correlation between board games and learning to read. Left-to-right and up-and-down motions that are part of these games help reading correlation. The games we produce are all over the screen."

"Your idea has potential," Perry complimented, sipping on his mug of coffee. "Here's my monkey wrench into this particular problem. Board game software has already been created, why should we recreate the wheel?"

"Because we're not. What I'm proposing is using what we know about how children learn to read and adding in the elements that make Gameboys and computer games appealing to kids so that we can create exciting educational games. It's not a new concept. Add in the No Child Left Behind initiative and we've got a winner."

Stroking his chin, Kent added, "We would incur very little out-of-pocket expense because of the hype surrounding the initiative. It'll be a great marketing tool."

"Tell us more, Cynthia," Matthew stated, leaning more comfortably in his chair.

"I've started working on some software called Alien Invader. It uses all the elements that we discussed earlier and I'm receiving input from some kids at a logic charter school. They've had some really great ideas for the program."

"Cool," Jacob muttered, fingering the wrapper from his health bar. "That's a smart move. Field help."

"Lisa has worked up estimates on how much this project may cost," Cynthia said. "I'll let her take over for now."

Lisa stood, took the remote from Cynthia, and selected a different set of slides.

Cynthia returned to her chair, happy that Matthew was open to a new project. Days like this made it a joy to come to work. Software would be created to not only entertain, but also educate the kids. If the project took off the way Cynthia hoped, this division would be a shining addition to Games People Play.

Matthew stood in the entrance to Cynthia's cubicle, leaning against the wall. He smiled approvingly at Cynthia and Lisa. "Congratulations. You ladies pulled off a great presentation today."

"Yes, congratulations." Lisa gave her friend the thumbs-up gesture. "I thought you were great."

"So were you." Cynthia touched Lisa's hand. "Many thanks for getting that financial stuff together. That helped clinch the deal."

Grinning, Lisa answered, "Thanks. I was scared to death."

"I don't believe it. You fielded the questions like you had all the answers within your grasp. I was proud of both of you." Mathew strolled into the room and stood behind Lisa. He placed a caressing hand on her shoulder.

"Lee, why don't we celebrate? I'll take you ladies to lunch. Your choice."

Lisa squirmed away from Matthew, saying, "I'm going to have to bow out on lunch. I've got a few things I need to finish."

Matthew flashed a persuasive smile at Lisa. "Come on, Lee. I'm the boss. The stuff you need to finish can wait."

She rose from her chair and hurried to the entrance. "No. My desk is covered with stuff I need to finish and I really want to clear as much off as possible. You and Cynthia go and enjoy. See you guys later."

Matthew's face was a mask of conflicting emotions. Frustration, pain, and anger skipped across his face.

"I'm sorry. Be patient," Cynthia whispered.

Chapter 8

Cynthia picked up the telephone to call Lisa, then replaced it. She sighed. Lisa volunteered at the hospital on Saturday mornings. Cynthia might have better luck reaching her if she waited until after three.

The doorbell rang and she wondered who would be visiting her. Hurrying down the hall, she opened the door and smiled. "Hi, Miss Helen, Mr. Nick. Come on in."

It had always amazed her how different they were. Mr. Nick's Hawaiian shirt and knee-length shorts immediately made Cynthia think that he'd been at the park enjoying an afternoon of sun and fresh air. She could imagine him playing football with his sons. Sometimes she found it hard to believe that this man, with the face of a bulldog and the rough voice of a coach, taught preschool and kindergarten.

In contrast, Miss Helen was dressed in a flowing ankle-length floral dress. The icy blue flowers emphasized her gray-streaked dark hair. She looked cool, professional, but approachable. She had an air that made you believe that you could depend on her. Miss Helen looked exactly like what she was, a high school principal.

Brown paper bags rattled, drawing Cynthia's gaze away from their faces and to the items in their hands. "What's all that?"

Stepping into the apartment, Miss Helen hugged Cynthia, then turned discreetly to appraise the younger woman. "Nick and I were at the farmers' market this morning and we thought you might appreciate a few pieces of fruit and some vegetables."

They were so thoughtful. "Thank you."

"You're welcome." With a wink, Miss Helen said, "I know you love strawberries and we found a great deal on them."

Giggling, Cynthia agreed. "You've got me on that one."

Miss Helen lifted a bag in her arms. "Do you want to got through the stuff with me and pick out what you want?"

"Yeah, sure." Cynthia took the other bag from Mr. Nick and started for the kitchen. "Come on, Miss Helen. Let's see what goodies you've got."

"My name is Mom and I'd like you to use it."

"M-M-Mom," Cynthia stammered, then sighed. "I'm sorry."

"Don't worry." Miss Helen touched her hand. "It'll come easier with time."

David's father stood uncomfortably in the hall with his hands in his pockets, shifting from one foot to the other. Cynthia heard the faint jiggle of coins from his pocket. "Can I get you anything, Mr. Nick?"

He pointed toward the living room and said in his rough, booming voice, "If you don't mind, I'm going to go sit and watch TV while you two ladies talk."

"Sure. The remote is on the coffee table." A few seconds later, she heard the ESPN announcer giving baseball scores.

Working in silence, Miss Helen unpacked half of the groceries while Cynthia stored them in the refrigerator. After placing a bag of apples in the fruit bin, she washed the strawberries in the sink and drained them on paper towels. Cynthia turned to the older woman and crossed her arms over her chest. With raised eyebrows and a question in her voice, she asked, "Talk?"

Sighing, Miss Helen turned to her, stroking her arm in a gentle, caring manner. "There are a couple of things I wanted to say to you. So many things happened at the party that I didn't get to talk to you that night. One, I want to welcome you to the family. And let you know how excited Nick and I are to have you finally become a permanent part of our lives."

Hugging her, Cynthia fought back tears. It meant so much to have Miss Helen's support. Miss Helen took Cynthia's hands and examined her. "How have you been? Any morning sickness or cravings?"

Shrugging, she answered, "No, I thought I would start to see a little weight gain by now. I haven't."

"This is a first baby and they tend to have their own agenda." She gave Cynthia a second hug. "Sweetie, don't worry about a thing. It's still early, you have plenty of time to pick up the twenty to twenty-five pounds you'll probably gain. Give it time."

Rolling her eyes, Cynthia muttered good-naturedly, "That's for sure."

"On a different note, I know it's easy to feel as if you're all alone. I've had five kids and maybe I can answer any questions or concerns you might have." She offered Cynthia a strawberry. "Your doctor will provide most of the answers you need. Thoughts will come to mind that you'll want to ask a person who has had the same experiences. I'm here for you. Okay?"

Cynthia took the strawberry and bit into it. "Thank you," she muttered, chewing the tart but juicy fruit.

"Right now I am going to pry. I saw your expression when David announced that you were getting married. You weren't ready for a public announcement, were you?"

Embarrassed, Cynthia looked away and hid her trembling hands behind her back. "No, at least, not yet."

"Why?" Miss Helen's voice softened, maintaining a nonintrusive air. "You don't think we're judging you, do you? Because we're not."

She turned to Miss Helen. "Oh, I know you aren't. Not at all. You've always been great to me. But there's so much going on between David and me; plus I'm nervous about the baby. How it's going to change our lives and if we're ready for it."

Miss Helen laughed. "Sweetie, babies change everyone's life. It's going to be okay. There's more, isn't there?"

"Some. I feel David wants to take over and control our lives. I don't feel like a partner anymore. We've always made decisions together, worked on situations as a team. This time he seems to be working solo and the baby and I are along for the ride."

Tapping a finger against her lips, her future mother-in-law said, "Tell me more."

Cynthia blew out a hot puff of air. This was David's mother and she didn't want to cause a conflict between David and his parents. "There are things we have to work out. Like where we're going to live and my job before we make further plans."

"Cynthia, part of what you're dealing with is the impending changes in the lifestyle that you and David are accustomed to. There are careers, households, and now a baby to consider. I'm sure it all seems overwhelming. You guys have never had to deal with these kinds of problems."

That's for sure, Cynthia thought, nibbling on another strawberry.

"Here's my advice. Sit down and tell him what's going on in your head. I know my son can be bullheaded and stubborn at times. This is where you have to make yourself heard over his ideas. If you want me or Nick to talk with him, we'll be happy to. But I believe you should try to talk to him first." Miss Helen wrapped a hand around Cynthia's shoulders and hugged her against her side. "Remember, Nick and I are here for you. We'll help in any way that we can." She touched Cynthia's cheek. "I want my daughter-in-law's happiness as much as my son's. You're family. Don't forget it."

"I won't."

"Good." Her head tilted as she considered another thought. "How far along are you? You don't look as if you've gained an ounce."

"About six weeks."

"I think Nick and I are going to work on fattening you up. We want a big, fat, healthy baby for you and David."

Laughing, Cynthia shook her head. "Not too big, I hope. The doctor's already warned me about overeating. Don't help," she admonished her good-naturedly.

"We can always bring you healthy stuff. Don't be surprised to see us next Saturday with another bag of goodies."

Cynthia entered Dr. Noah's office with trepidation. She'd received a message from his staff, requesting that she come into the office to have blood drawn. What in the heck was going on?

The late afternoon sun cast a shadow over the empty waiting room. She hurried to the reception window. "Hi, April."

The receptionist gave her a welcoming smile. A white uniform peeked from under a blue, green, and yellow paisley smock. "Come on through, Miss Williams. Dr. Noah wants the technician to draw another tube of blood and we will also need a urine sample."

Cynthia nodded, waiting for her chance to ask a question or two.

"He also wants to speak with you before you leave."

"Okay. Do you know what this is all about?"

"No, I don't have any info. I'm sure Dr. Noah will explain everything once you've completed the samples."

Cynthia rolled her eyes. April's nonanswer didn't relieve any of her worry.

Twenty minutes later, she sat in one of the two chairs facing Dr. Noah's desk, waiting for him. Chewing on her bottom lip, she glanced around his office. The light blue walls were lined with degrees and the bookshelves contained medical texts and journals.

One book in particular, *Problem Pregnancies,* drew her attention. Her stomach twisted into a knot. Maybe that was why he asked her to return for more tests. She shot a silent prayer to God for guidance.

Dr. Noah entered the office with his lab coat billowing and a manila file under his arm. A beige shirt, brown, red, and orange tie, and chocolate-brown trousers were visible from the coat's opening. "Sorry you had to wait. I had to slip over to the hospital to check on a patient."

"That's fine. I've got to tell you, you've got me really worried. What's going on?"

"Calm down," he offered in a soothing tone. "Don't be upset."

She stood, planting her hands on his desk. "Well, I am upset. You leave a messaging saying I need to come into the office as soon as possible. Trust me, all kinds of health problems flew through my mind."

He patted her hand, indicating that she should

have a seat, and sat behind his desk. "Let's talk. First, I have to apologize for taking so long getting your original test results. We sent our requests to an outside lab and they took a few days to evaluate your specimens."

"Okay," she muttered, waiting for him to hit her with the big stuff. "What is this about?"

"Your blood test came back negative." He opened the file and removed a piece of paper, turning it to face her.

"Negative? How could that be? Are you saying I'm not pregnant?" She picked up the lab report, scanning the information, hoping to learn more about what was going on. Several items were highlighted, but none of them made any sense to her. "What does this mean?"

"Your hormones are elevated."

"Is that normal for a pregnant woman?"

"There has been a shift in your hormones, which indicates that you are not pregnant. We have to find out what's going on and why your tests are coming back this way."

"Dr. Noah, I'm completely baffled." She raised a hand and let it drop into her lap. "I don't know what to tell my fiancé. Honestly, I'm not sure what you are trying to tell me."

"I'm saying that we need to do another round of blood work to make sure you're pregnant. I've also scheduled an ultrasound for you to determine what's going on. If you have time, you can have one done today. At this point there's nothing to tell your fiancé. As I've said, hormones are present and you indicate the symptoms of pregnancy. Should your blood test or ultrasound come back with negative results, then we'll take the next step and try to figure out what's going on. Until I say otherwise, treat this as a pregnancy and I want you to continue with your vitamin regimen and all the precautions we discussed at your last visit."

"If I'm not pregnant, what am I?" Cynthia's forehead crinkled as she tried to absorb what Dr. Noah had told her.

"I don't know yet. But I will find out. Can you do the ultrasound today?" he asked again.

She rose from her chair. "Sure, Dr. Noah. I guess there's no time like the present."

He stood and patted her hand reassuringly. "I'm sorry that I don't have better news or more information. We'll figure this out and get everything on track for you. I promise. April will tell you where to go for the ultrasound."

"Okay," she answered meekly, making her way out of the office. She needed to talk with somebody. David was out of the question because of his most recent case. She didn't want to burden him. Miss Helen would have been nice to talk to, she thought. Maybe she should call Lisa. They hadn't talked privately since David announced their engagement and she had always been a good listener.

Cynthia climbed into her queen-size brass bed in a pair of mint-green pajama bottoms and matching T-strapped top. She glanced at the clock, then reached for the telephone and dialed Lisa's home number. The phone rang several times before her voice mail kicked in. "Hi. This is Lisa and I'm in the middle of something right now. Leave a message and I'll get back with you."

She was just getting used to the idea of a baby and now the doctor was saying that there might not be one. That idea scared her. Cynthia wanted this baby.

She needed to talk with her friend. Get her opinion on her test results and hopefully get some reassurance. Where was she? It was after ten o'clock and tomorrow was a workday.

"Hi, it's Cynthia. I wanted to touch base and see how things are going for you and talk about what's going on with me. If you get in before eleven, give me a call. I'll be up. Bye."

Cynthia felt as if she spent more time talking to Lisa's voice mail than she did talking to her friend. She understood that Matthew was part of Lisa's life now, but she still wished she could get a little of Lisa's time.

Maybe tomorrow Lisa would be available for lunch, then Cynthia could talk about her concerns.

Chapter 9

"You wanted to see me?" Simon Broderick asked from David Daniels's doorway.

"Yeah." David rose from his chair, stepped around his desk, and met the other man at the door. Shaking hands, he said, "Thanks for coming."

A moment of uncertainty made David question his plan. He wanted to make things easier for Cynthia by taking the stress and worry off her shoulders and placing them on his, smoothing the way for her. Could this act of kindness come back to bite him squarely in the butt? he wondered.

Simon strolled across the room with a hand in his pocket. "No problem, although I must admit I'm a bit confused."

"I'll explain everything. Come on in."

David led the man back to his desk and patted the chair reserved for a guest. "Have a seat. Can I get you anything? Cup of coffee, soft drink, juice?"

Simon shook his head, silently examining David's office. "I'm fine."

He returned to his place behind the desk, sat, and studied Simon. The five-foot-ten investigator had the quiet, unassuming looks that worked well with someone who needed to blend into an array of different environments. Round-faced, mouse-brown hair, clean-shaven, green eyes that were unremarkable. Invisible unless he needed not to be. Simon was perfect as a private investigator.

Simon finished his sweep of the office, then turned to David. *Observant, that is good*, David thought.

"What can I do for you?" He crossed his right leg over his left knee and tugged on the hem of his gabardine trousers.

"I have a job for you."

His eyebrows lifted a fraction and his voice held a trace of suspicion. "Don't you have an investigator on your team?"

"Yes, I do. This job is separate from the work you do for the firm." David rubbed the pads of his fingers together before placing his elbows on the desk.

"Oh?"

"Yes." This point needed to be made perfectly clear, no misunderstandings. You'll work on it on your own time, after hours. Also, I'll pay you directly. There won't be any conflict of interest or connection with the firm."

"Could there be?"

"Be what?"

"A conflict of interest?"

"I doubt it," David answered. "This is personal and there's nothing illegal about what I'm asking you to do."

"I'm not going to say yes until I hear the details," Simon stated evenly.

"Fair enough."

"It may not be anything I want to do."

"I don't want it to spill over into your job and I don't want to hear about it through the office grapevine." David held the other man's gaze. "Understood?"

"Got it. Whatever I do has to be after hours and silent to the office."

"Good."

"What's the job?"

David rose from his chair and moved around to the front of his desk. He sat on the edge and rested his hands on his thighs. A faint scent of citrus touched his nostrils. "My fiancée's mother dropped her in the foster care system when she was a baby. Cynthia has never heard from the woman. We have no idea who she is or even if the woman is still alive."

"Intriguing. Go on."

"I want you to locate her and find out all the information you can. Give it to me and I'll decide what I want to do with it after that."

"Shouldn't I be talking with your fiancée?"

"No. I don't want her to get her hopes up and then find this woman to be a people user or worse."

"I've done cases like this before. Generally, they don't turn out too pretty," Simon warned.

"That's what I'm afraid of. My fiancée is afraid to admit that she wants to know her mother. She's using the excuse that she needs the medical history. I want to know everything before we contact this woman and let her into our lives."

"Wise choice."

"Are you interested in the case?"

Simon leaned back in his chair and regarded David with a keen eye. Nodding, he said, "Yes, I am."

"Good." David rose and returned to his chair. He opened his desk drawer and removed his checkbook. With a pen in one hand, he glanced at Simon. "What's your daily rate?"

Stroking his chin, Simon smiled. Dollar signs flashed in his green eyes. David knew this wouldn't be cheap. He'd pay any price to make sure that Cynthia felt more comfortable with their future and the baby's.

"This is after hours, so it's going to cost more. We haven't discussed travel. How do you want to handle things if I need to go out of town? Who's going to pay for that?"

"I'll cover everything. What's your rate?" David asked.

"Three-five-zero per night, plus expenses."

David filled out the check, ripped it from the book, and handed it to Simon. "Done."

Simon glanced at the scrap of paper, folded it in half, and placed it inside his breast pocket. "I need details." He removed a small spiral notebook and pen from the same pocket.

"Here's everything we know," David said, reaching across his desk for a typed sheet of paper. "This is her mother's name and last known address. That address is more than twenty-five years old, though. I don't think you'll get anything from that." He handed Simon the list.

Simon took the sheet, skimming the information. "You never know. Could be that one of her family members still lives there. I won't know till I check it out."

"I included the address and contact person from the foster care agency, plus Cynthia's foster parents. They're a decent couple. If they can help, they will. Any information they have, they'll give you without much trouble."

"What about a Social Security number? I might be able to track the mom from that."

David blew out a puff of air. "I don't have it. Check with the foster parents or the agency. They may have it. Who knows? They may know how to get it."

"What about your fiancée? Can I talk to her?"

"No."

"I might need her," Simon pushed.

Standing, David shoved his hands inside the pockets of his trousers and glanced out the twenty-eighth-floor window. He didn't want Cynthia to worry about this. If it all worked out, he'd present her with a wonderful wedding present. But this could be a recipe for unpleasantness. So far, Latonya Williams hadn't shown the slightest interest in her daughter. And there might be a good reason for that. He didn't want to see the woman he loved hurt by the callousness of her mother. Cynthia didn't need to know this was happening until the proper time presented itself, he'd figured.

"Come through me. I don't want her to know I'm doing this. I want to be certain of this woman's motives before I tell my fiancée."

"You're the boss." Simon removed the check

from his pocket and glanced at it a second time. "You've paid me for a week. What if it takes longer? How long do you want me to continue?"

"Until I tell you to stop."

"It's your world, boss. With the firm, I write up a weekly status report. You want the same treatment?"

"No, verbal's fine. Just give me a call when you find something signicant."

Simon rose, shook hands with David, and handed him his business card. "Thanks for the job. If you come up with anything more, call. My home and cell numbers are on there," he said, indicating the slip of paper.

"Thanks for the help."

David watched Simon leave his office. He hoped he was doing the right thing. He understood Cynthia's dilemma and wanted to be her knight in shining armor. But maybe digging into the past was the wrong thing to do. What if Cynthia's mother didn't want to be found and his snooping complicated things? What then? He figured he'd deal with it when Simon found her.

Autumn Snyder stepped into David's office and shut the door after her. She looked ready to explode. Long, red, wavy hair framed her soft ivory skin and partially hid her flushed cheeks. Her almond-shaped blue eyes sparkled with excitement.

From his desk, David asked, "What's up?"

"Old man Ruffino is on his way down here."

"For what?"

"I don't know. But your secretary got a call from Ruffino's secretary wanting to make sure you were in the office. Maybe this has something to do with your making partner."

David shook his head. "No. The bigwigs would call me up to them. They wouldn't come down here."

Visibly disappointed, Autumn pouted.

David opened his mouth to remind her that nothing had been settled regarding the new partner position, but the telephone intercom rang. He picked up the phone. "Yes, Linda?"

"Dave, Mr. Ruffino is here to see you."

"Send him in."

David straightened his gray silk tie and reached for his charcoal suit jacket. Whatever situation brought Ruffino here, David wanted to provide his most professional impression. Hurrying across his office, he opened the door and found the tall, white-haired Italian waiting on the opposite side.

"Hello, Mr. Ruffino. Come on in." David extended a hand.

Ruffino grabbed his hand and shook it. He strolled into the room, examining his surroundings, moving around the desk to look out the floor-to-ceiling window. "It's Mario. Call me Mario."

Eyebrows raised, David observed Ruffino.

"Mario." Cupping Autumn's elbow, David led her to the older man. "This is my law clerk. Mario Ruffino, Autumn Snyder."

Mario took Autumn's hand and shook it firmly.

David moved back toward his desk. "Can I get you anything?"

"No. Nothing."

"Then have a seat and tell me what I can do for you." David patted the visitor's chair on his way to his chair.

Ruffino settled into the chair, drawing his navy jacket around him. "We have a case that we want you to handle."

Eyebrows arched, David repeated, "We?"

Ruffino cleared his throat. "The senior partners and I," he added.

David nodded, waiting for Ruffino to elaborate. Autumn stood behind Ruffino, holding her breath.

"I'm sure you've read in the papers about Dytech Technologies."

Again, David nodded. Dytech was a very high-profile case.

"They've contacted our office regarding representation. They are under investigation for possible embezzlement from the company's pension fund."

David remained silent, waiting for more information.

"You'll be the lead on this case."

That was the last thing he expected. *But why me?* David's eyes narrowed as he absorbed this information.

"The firm will give you everything you need, staff, an investigator. Anything, name it. It's yours."

"Doesn't Dytech have company attorneys?"

"Yes, they do. But they want someone removed from everything that's going on in that office to work on it. Dytech's attorneys will be available for consultations, of course, but you would run the case and the investigation."

"Intriguing."

"It can be."

"Why are you handing this case to me?"

"Because of the publicity. Dytech is fighting two battles, one in court and another in the media. That's one of the reasons they are seeking outside representation. Now, about you." He settled his laced hands in his lap. "You have one of the most impressive records with this firm. In the three years you've been with us, you've lost only seven of eighty-five cases. And you know how to handle the media. That's a powerful combination and one Dytech is willing to pay for."

David leaned back in his chair, studying old man Ruffino. There must be a hidden agenda, but what was it? "This case will take up a great deal of my time. Are you asking me to add this to my case-load?"

Ruffino shook his white hair and stretched his long legs in front of him. "No. We're going to have one of the other attorneys take over your cases so that you can concentrate exclusively on Dytech. I don't have to tell you how important this is. It's imperative you give it your all."

"All my cases get everything I have."

Ruffino raised a hand. "Sorry, I didn't mean to imply anything else. Let me explain. The senior partners and I have followed your career and we believe you are the attorney to handle this case. You're young, aggressive, and thorough. That's why you were elected. You don't stop until you get it done. And I like that. Plus, you know as well as I do that this is a career-making case."

The old man had placed his cards on the table and there was little question about his motive. "You're ambitious. This case will make you."

"It's tempting, but I don't see how I can do it. I mean I have several cases that are going to explode any minute. Turning everything over to someone else doesn't feel like the appropriate or responsible thing to do."

Mario's description of the case made it sound like something he could handle. Unfortunately, there were more issues to consider. Cynthia and the baby needed him. He didn't want to be away from home at this time. On the other hand, this could be the case that put him in a corner office as a partner.

"If you'd like, you can still oversee those cases. But you must focus on Dytech. They will be paying your salary until the case is completed. Dytech is the one that can propel you into partner status."

"Are you ordering me to take this case?"

"No. It's a choice. But I recommend that you consider your future and career."

"Why don't you tell me more?"

"Gary Jorworsky is one of the new breed of millionaires. You know the type. He started in his basement and took his company national. About three years ago, he decided to expand. Well, at the same time, someone took advantage of the pension fund and stole from it. The media has fried Jorworsky. But we're going to prove them wrong."

Keeping his face a blank mask, David listened as Ruffino explained some of the other details related to the case. Here was an opportunity to shine and move closer to that partner's position he coveted.

He didn't have any doubt. He knew he'd take the case. And he'd win it.

Excited, Autumn practically jumped up and down the minute Ruffino left the office. David stood at his doorway, watching the young law clerk.

"We've got a nationally known case. This is going to make my career." Autumn rubbed her hands together and walked across the room to his desk.

For a beat, David remained silent. "You're right."

"Hey. You don't seem excited at all. What gives?" She moved to within inches of him and grabbed his arm. She flashed him a hundred-watt smile. "You're going to make partner," she sang. "And when I get my degree, I'll be a permanent member of your team."

"You're plowing way ahead of things."

"No, I'm not." She flung her arms around him and squeezed. "We're going to be rich."

David heard the door open and shut. He looked up and found Cynthia in his office. His heart stopped in his chest, then started beating again.

"Well, hello, attorney Dave." She folded her arms across her chest.

Chapter 10

"Did I come at a bad time?" Cynthia eyed David for several long seconds before turning her attention to the woman in his arms. She was a tiny thing, standing no more than five feet tall with a round face, straight nose, delicate white skin, and bright blue eyes. Cynthia willed herself not to jump to any conclusions.

David's hands dropped and he took a step away, heading across the room to where Cynthia stood. "Hey, sweetheart."

Cynthia smiled through a rising tide of anger. Her hand was clutched tightly around the strap of her purse. "Is this a celebration?"

He rubbed the pads of his fingers together as he always did when he was nervous. "Little excitement, that's all. I just got a visit from old man Ruffino. You remember him?"

Cynthia nodded.

"Ruffino offered me a new case. A high-profile case. A career-making case," David emphasized.

She considered David's explanation for a moment and tilted her head in the redhead's direction. "Is this the client?"

He glanced over at the other woman, waving her over. "No. This is my law clerk, Autumn Snyder. You talked to her on the phone a couple of weeks ago. Autumn, come meet my fiancée."

"You called one day, looking for David," Autumn explained. "I mean, Mr. Daniels. You two had an appointment and he was at a deposition. Remember?"

"That was you?"

"Yes, indeed."

"Now that everyone knows each other, let me do the formal introductions." David waved a hand in Cynthia's direction. "Autumn, this is Cynthia Williams. Cynthia, Autumn Snyder."

"Nice to meet you in person," Autumn said in a perky tone, offering a hand.

The two women shook hands.

David studied Cynthia. "What brings you here? You all right?"

"I'm fine. We need to talk about Lisa."

"Lisa?"

Cynthia nodded.

David tapped his lips with a finger. "Cyn, give me a minute, will you? Why don't you sit at my desk? Are you hungry?"

She shook her head.

"I'll be right with you." He turned to Autumn. "Contact the team. Schedule a meeting for tomorrow at nine. I want to start working on this ASAP. Also, have Linda contact Ruffino's secretary and get all the files from his office."

Retrieving a notepad from the conference table,

she scribbled notes, nodding as she took down David's request. "Will do."

"See if you can schedule a conference call with the attorneys from Dytech, Autumn. We might as well get an idea of what they know right away."

"Any time? Day?"

"Within the week." He gazed out the window.

With a pen still posed to take more notes, Autumn asked, "Anything more?"

"No." David headed back to his desk. "That should get you started. When you contact Dytech, make sure you request any and all documentation they have: memos, letters, and spreadsheets, whatever. I want a list of employees dating back five years. Schedule a meeting with Dytech's attorneys after our team meets. If you need to reschedule some other stuff, do it."

"That's it?"

David nodded.

Autumn returned the cap to the pen, shoved it inside the pocket of her slacks, and called on her way out, "I'll e-mail you and let you know what I find out."

He sank into his chair, watching Cynthia. In turn, she studied him. Silence settled between them.

"I don't want to do the stare-down thing. So I'll go first," David said in a smooth but insistent tone. "You have the wrong impression. Autumn gets a wee bit excited, it was nothing more." He linked his fingers and laid his hands on the desk.

"I didn't say anything," Cynthia answered in a nonchalant tone.

"You don't have to. I know you. You're way too calm. What's up? Why are you here?"

Cynthia remained silent. She wanted to tell David about the blood test results but Dr. Noah seemed confident everything was fine. She blew out a deep sigh and returned her mind to Autumn. She seemed a bit too familiar with David for Cynthia's peace of mind. She turned to David. "Autumn's cute."

He scratched his head and in a cautious voice offered, "I guess. Maybe. I don't know. Autumn's a good employee."

Nodding, she answered in an even, nonaccusatory tone, "I saw that."

"What does that mean?" he asked, sipping on his coffee.

Shrugging, Cynthia linked her fingers and dropped them in her lap. "Nothing. Just, she's cute."

The expression in his eyes changed to that sexy glint, making her heart speed up. David rose, rounded the desk, and hunched down next to her chair. "Hey," he muttered in a silken tone. "Nobody is cuter than my girl." Taking her hand between both of his, he kissed the palm. "Nobody."

David's declaration warmed her heart. Stroking his cheek, Cynthia felt warm all over. He pulled her from the chair. His kiss brought passionate emotions to the surface. David stroked her wet lips with his tongue. "There's nobody in the world that I love more."

As always, he seemed to know what she needed

and made sure she got it. "That's what I wanted to hear," she confessed.

Slowly releasing her, he returned to his place behind the desk. "Now, what's going on with my sister?"

"Lots. But I want to ask you something else first."

He tossed a hand in the air. "Shoot."

"New case. Big case. What's that all about?"

"The Dytech pension fraud."

Her eyes grew large. She knew this was quite an extraordinary coup. "The one where they indicted the president for stealing from the employee pension fund?"

He nodded.

"That's the case they want you to take?"

"That's the one," David answered.

"Wow! Well, it sounds like that partner stuff is right around the corner." She grinned back at him. "Congratulations."

David chuckled. "That's what Autumn said. Don't get your hopes up; it's way too early to start counting my pennies."

"What do you think?"

"I think I'm in for a particularly difficult case. And I'm not certain of the outcome."

"Uncertain? You're going to win. Period. You're a great attorney. You'll do just fine."

"Thanks. I need a groupie."

"Hey." She lifted her hands in the air. "I'm your first adoring fan. Now here's the part I'm concerned with. What happens to our getting married in Vegas and all the plans we've made?"

David exhaled heavily and leaned back in his

chair. "Good question. And to be perfectly honest, I was considering the problem when old man Ruffino insisted I take the case."

"Insisted?"

He nodded.

"You mean, demanded?" Cynthia corrected, reaching across the desk to touch his hand.

He held her hand. "Yes. I didn't have any wiggle room. Cyn, I don't know how this case is going to affect our lives. I know the partners expect me to win. Which means I've got to put my all into it. But I don't want you to think that I didn't consider our life when he made the offer. You and the baby are my top priority."

"Can you win?"

"I don't know. I only know what Ruffino told me."

"There's a lot of pressure involved in this case."

"Tell me about it."

"Are you sure you can't hand it back to them?" Cynthia asked.

"Not this time."

"David, here's my take on this. They stole from the people who worked for them, left those poor people without a dollar to live on. It's not right."

He shook a finger in Cynthia's direction. "Sweetheart, we don't know that. That hasn't been proven yet."

"I know. But if they did, how can you justify defending them? I mean, your parents are getting closer to retirement age. How would you feel if Miss Helen and Mr. Nick found out that their pension funds had been stolen by their boss?"

"Calm down. Number one, my parents work for the board of education. Their pensions are safe. Number two, I can't make judgment calls like that. I have to go with the evidence. Now let's talk about something else."

"You're the attorney, so I'll leave you to it, but I'd feel real funny about things if I were in your place."

"That's why I'm Attorney Dave and you're Cynthia, video game software designer extraordinaire."

She bowed her head. "Thank you."

"What's up with my sister?" he asked.

"David, I'm worried that she's going to break her engagement."

He groaned.

"I don't know how to help her. Lisa's so lost. I caught up with her in her office today and when I tried to reason with her, she rejected all my suggestions."

He tapped a pen against the desk. "Maybe you're the wrong person to talk with her. How about Matthew? He has a vested interest in what happens."

"I ran into Matthew in Lisa's office. She was out to lunch so we spoke pretty candidly. He's worried and doesn't know what to do."

"I hate to bother Mom and Dad. Lisa is a grown woman. She can make her own decisions."

"I know. There are times in our lives when we can't see what's in front of us. For Lisa, that time is now. She needs a little help, figuring out her next move. I'm her friend and I want to be there for her."

"Okay, let's do this. Give her a few more days to

resolve things. If she's still in the same mind-set, we'll talk to her together."

"That's not a bad idea. What I haven't been able to do alone, might work if you're with me. Plus, seeing us as a couple might make her realize what she's giving up."

"It sounds like a plan."

Chapter 11

Cynthia glanced at her watch, shifted the batch of magazines into the crook of her right arm, then picked up her pace. She marched purposefully through the aisles, nodding at coworkers as she passed.

Lisa always went to lunch at noon; Cynthia wanted to catch her before she got out of the building. Since David announced their plans to get married, she and Lisa hadn't touched base. Wherever or whenever she tried to visit, Lisa made a point of being elsewhere.

Turning into Lisa's cubicle, Cynthia was disappointed to find she wasn't there again. Lately, that seemed to be the pattern of things between them. Now what? Cynthia drummed her nails against the desktop. She stepped around the workstation to place an array of bride magazines in the center of the desk. She opened Lisa's drawer and removed a yellow Post-it and a pen to leave a note.

Matthew hurried into the cubicle as she was writing, saying, "Lee? I thought we might do lunch."

"Hey," Cynthia greeted.

A shadow of disappointment passed over his face. "Sorry, Cynthia. I thought I might catch Lisa."

"Me too."

"Lisa's a bit slippery these days," he said mockingly.

She examined Matthew, debating whether she should ask him what was going on. His features were drawn. The happiness that had once been a part of him was conspicuously absent.

Striding across the room, he took the guest chair and leaned close to Cynthia to select a peppermint from the dish on Lisa's workstation. "How are you doing? You guys set a date yet?"

"We're talking about it. David wants as many members of his family as possible to go to Vegas with us. That's making it difficult."

Nodding, he unwrapped the mint and popped it in his mouth. "I can see that. What about you? Do you have any family that might want to come to your wedding?"

That's what I'm trying to find out, she thought. "Not really. I'm a product of the foster care system."

Matthew nodded solemnly.

"What about you and my girl? How are your wedding plans coming?" Cynthia wiped a small particle of dust from her glasses, then returned them to her face.

He sighed, pinching the bridge of his nose with two fingers. "That's a good question."

Her eyebrows crinkled a bit. "What do you mean?" She was certain his answer wouldn't make her a happy camper.

"Since the day you announced your engagement,

I haven't been able to get her to open up. She shuts down and I can't find anything that will get her to talk about what's going on in her head." There was a faint tremor in his voice as though he was touched by some strong emotions. "To be honest, I've been debating the possibility of talking to Mr. and Mrs. Daniels. They may be able to offer some advice," he added in a tired voice. "I'm at a loss."

Cynthia listened to Matthew with a heavy heart. This baby thing was still straining a relationship too new to handle such a major complication.

"Don't forget, she comes from a close-knit clan that believes in children and family. I'm sure it's the baby thing again. I mean, I know you guys are checking with specialists. But Lisa has always wanted children. When we were kids, she always wanted to be the mom when we played house."

"I see your point." He tented his fingers together. "I know it's the baby thing. I thought we had put it behind us when she finally agreed to marry me. I guess it's like your shadow, it's behind you, but you can't get rid of it. Now everything's mucked up. I don't know how to convince her that we'll be okay. That we can have a good life together with or without babies."

"David announcing that I'm pregnant didn't help. It kicked her right out of the safe little haven you'd created. Just remember, this is Lisa's MO. When she can't cope with things, she withdraws. After Jenn announced she was pregnant, Lisa shunned everyone. She made excuse after excuse to stay away from family functions. I was really worried about her."

He leaned forward. "What happened? How did you get things to turn around?" he asked with an eager tone to his voice.

"It took weeks and lots of e-mails to get Lisa to admit how upset she felt and then it took an additional couple of weeks to convince her to come back to the family." Her lips twitched with humor. "When she kept ignoring my messages, I sent my secret weapon to her apartment."

"Secret weapon?" He laughed richly, folding his arms across his chest.

"Yeah. I sent David to talk with her."

"Did it work?"

"Yes." She smiled smugly.

He let out a great round of laughter. The hearty sound rippled through the small cubicle. "Excellent. I might have to hire him for a few days."

Cynthia held up a hand to silence him. "Seriously, you've got a hard road ahead. Don't give up."

"No can do. I love her too much." He spoke with quiet, determined firmness.

"Good. This might sound like a cliché, but it's true. Lisa's worth it. And I truly believe you guys belong together. Hold firm. It'll work out."

"What about you? Has Lisa cut you off without a word."

"I haven't heard from her in weeks. She doesn't return my calls. Normally, we do lunch together at least three times a week. I can't catch her to arrange anything."

"Is there anything I can do to help?"

"Maybe you shouldn't do anything. I'll talk with

her." Cynthia smoothed her loose locks of hair into place. "I mean, she used to tell me everything."

"If you can get her to open up, you'd have my thanks. You might get a raise."

"Bribery. Sweet. Can I have that part in writing?"

"No."

Matthew rose and glanced around Lisa's cubicle. "There's no point in me hanging around. Chances are she'll wait until I leave before sneaking back into her office anyway. I need to get back and get some work done."

"Give her some time, a little space, and let me talk to her. We can turn this around," she encouraged in a soft, understanding voice. "I know we can."

"I hope you're right. I appreciate the help. Thanks, Cynthia." Matthew squeezed her hand before leaving.

Cynthia sat at Lisa's desk, finishing her note, when her friend finally waltzed into the room. Dressed in a tailored rust-colored jacket and matching capri pants, Lisa looked attractive and cool. In contrast, Cynthia felt fat and dumpy in a pair of black Dockers and a white blouse.

"Oh!" Lisa dropped a brown paper bag on her desk. Embarrassed, she muttered, "Hi, Cyn."

"Hey, hey, now. I haven't talked to you in a while. How you be?" she asked, lacing her fingers together.

"Good. And you?"

"The same. You just missed Matthew."

Lisa glanced over her shoulder. "Oh. I'll call him a little later."

Cynthia turned the bag to reveal the restaurant's name. "Wong's? Mmm. You should have called me. I would have loved a couple of spring rolls."

Moving across the cubicle, Lisa sat next to the desk, while Cynthia remained seated behind it. "It came up out of the blue. You remember Felicia from human resources?"

Cynthia nodded.

"She called me and asked me to lunch, so I picked up my purse and headed out the door."

"I see." Cynthia studied her friend for several silent moments. She smiled, laying her hand on the stack of magazines. "I stopped at Waldenbooks a couple of nights ago and I couldn't resist picking up a few bride magazines for you."

"Oh. That's nice. Thank you." Lisa glanced at the magazines.

Cynthia flipped through one and tapped a page with her finger. "Here's some really good stuff about honeymoons, church selections, and reception hall decorations. Stuff you and Matthew are going to need." She pushed the magazines in Lisa's direction.

"Thanks again." Lisa waved the magazines away without touching them. "I'll take a look at them later."

Cynthia inhaled deeply and tried again. "Make sure you let Matthew get a look-see at the article about honeymoons. By the way, have you guys decided on your locale?"

Lisa shrugged, showing more interest in the messages she sifted through than her plans for her wedding. "We haven't talked about it. I'm sure he has something in mind. After all, the honeymoon is the male thing."

"Actually, it's for both of you. Think about it, you don't want him to choose a place that you don't want to go to, do you?"

Waving away the topic, Lisa said, "Pfff. Let's talk about something else. How about your wedding plans? You all set for Vegas?"

"We're still trying to coordinate the family's schedule."

"It should be fairly easy. All the teaching folks are on summer break until the end of August."

Cynthia laughed. "You would think so. But it's not the case. J.D.'s the only one that can make it without a hitch. Your mother has a bunch of meetings scheduled during the summer and she can't get out of them."

"That's Ma."

She reached across the desk and asked in a somber tone, "So what's going on with you, Lisa? You don't seem happy about your engagement and, frankly, neither does Matthew. Is everything okay between you two?"

"We're fine. I think we're going through an adjustment phase," she answered in a wintry tone. The ice off her words could chill a scalding cup of green tea.

"Lisa, remember how you reacted when Jenn first told the family that she was pregnant?"

Staring at the wall, Lisa remained stubbornly silent.

"We talked a lot before you could bring yourself to attend family functions. Now it's me that's having the baby and I don't want your niece or nephew to come between you and me. We've been friends far too long for things to change between us now. Besides, I need your support through this."

"I don't know where you got the idea that I'm having a problem with you and the baby. It's just not true," Lisa replied through stiff lips.

"Really? How come every time I call or suggest lunch you can't seem to find the time? Have I done something to offend you—"

"Of course not," Lisa snapped, facing Cynthia directly for the first time. "There are so many things going on right now. I haven't had time to get together with you."

"Right." Cynthia's voice hardened. "Don't give me this crap. If you are having problems with the baby and me or with Matthew, I'm here to listen. I want to help in any way I can. Lisa, you and I have been friends since the seventh grade. I've always been straight with you and I expect the same. But I can't help unless you're willing to tell me the truth."

Lisa squeezed her eyes shut and turned away, twisting the engagement ring around her finger. "You're mistaken. There's nothing wrong between you and me."

"There must be something else. Is it Matthew? Are you getting cold feet? Are you afraid of the baby thing? I know for a fact that it doesn't matter to Matthew. He wants to be with you, no matter what."

A tear slid down Lisa's cheek as she answered in a tiny, confused voice, "It matters to me. Nobody understands that I want a family that includes children."

"What about adoption? I mean, look at me. I could have benefited from adopted parents."

"It's not the same," Lisa answered, choking back tears.

"It can be if you want it to be. Loving a child doesn't change whether you give birth to it or not." Cynthia rose, hurried around the desk, and placed an arm around Lisa. "Don't give up. You can't predict the future. All you can do is live your life right now. Give it all you've got."

"You have no idea what I'm going through." Lisa brushed away her tears with the back of her hand.

"I know you're hurting, badly. I know that you love Matthew. So what's the problem? Let him love you back. Don't throw everything away. Please, don't do that."

Lisa pulled herself together and wiped away her tears. "Look, I'm sorry. I didn't mean to do this. Sometimes things get a bit overwhelming and I don't know what to do. I'm okay."

"No, you're not." Cynthia squeezed her friend's hand. "And you're not alone, either. Whether you believe me or not, I'm here for you."

"Can we drop the subject? I don't want to talk about it anymore."

"For now. But talk to Matthew. Let him know how you're feeling. He needs to understand what's going on in your head. You need to let him in. Talk and let things happen naturally from that point. Promise me you'll do that."

Lisa wiped away her tears with a Kleenex and shook her head. "I can't. At least not yet."

"When?"

"I don't know. I need more time to work things out in my head."

"Right now you're scaring that man something terrible. Matthew is all tensed up because he thinks you're going to call off the wedding any day now. Don't do that to him, please. Talk to him first."

"I'll think about it. That's the best I can give you."

"No problem." Cynthia reached for the Wong's take-out bag, opening it she glanced at her friend. "Any spring rolls in here?"

Chapter 12

Cynthia wiped her mouth with her napkin after devouring her grilled chicken sandwich and found Jacob's eyes on her. "What?" She picked up her glass of lemonade.

"You enjoy your food." Jacob's sun-leathered face split into a grin as he pushed the remains of his Greek salad toward the center of the table.

"I seem to be a bottomless pit these days. Must be the pregnancy," she said in self-mocking tones. She realized then that she still hadn't told anyone about her negative blood work. What was the sense in getting everyone riled up for nothing?

He laughed and leaned back in the booth. "Maybe so."

Searching for their server, Cynthia gazed longingly at the counter loaded with specialty cheesecakes and licked her lips. "I still have room for a piece of cheesecake."

He waved a hand toward the dessert counter. "Indulge yourself."

"In a minute," she answered, turning away from the goodies with a reluctant sigh. "I'm sure you have better things to do besides watching me eat for fifteen minutes. You're on the clock. I don't want to keep you, so why don't we get on with the interview?"

"I'm fine. Don't worry about me." He poured additional hot tea into his mug and the fragrance of peppermint filled the small booth. "I've actually enjoyed watching a woman eat instead of picking at her food. It's good to see someone with a healthy appetite."

"I don't know how healthy it is. But I do enjoy my food."

Jacob pulled a Palm Pilot from his pocket and switched it on. He removed the black plastic pointer and touched the screen with the tip. "Let's start with some basic info." He studied the illuminated screen for several long moments before speaking. "Do you know if you or your parents are originally from Chicago? When did your mother leave you with the foster care agency? If you have it, I need the date. How old were you? Do you have your mother's full name? And what about your father? Do you have any information about him?"

Cynthia felt her stomach churn. There was so much that she didn't know about where she came from and who she was. "I'm not sure about some of the facts. But I'll give you the information that I have."

"That's what I need. Tell me what you know or remember. Once I start digging, we'll compare details and you'll have all the answers.

"My foster parents, the Grants, told me they got me when I was about eight months old. My mother was single and couldn't take care of me, so she left me with the agency."

Nodding, Jacob listened without making comments. His passive mask hid all thoughts from her.

Nervously, she ran her fingers through her hair. "My mother's full name is Latonya Williams. I know nothing about my father, not even his name." She looked away as heat rushed into her cheeks. That was another item that made her feel alone. She didn't have a connection to her father, either.

Jacob reached across the table and gently folded her hand within his. She flinched, pulling away. Something in his eyes made her question his motives.

"It's not your fault. Don't accept your parents' mistakes as yours," he reassured her softly.

With an uncomfortable smile on her lips, Cynthia shifted around in her seat, rubbing her hand against her skirt. "Thank you."

"Don't thank me yet. I want to help. Keep talking. What else do you know? Do you have grandparents?" he asked.

"Why would you ask that? If I don't have parents, why would I know anything about my grandparents?"

Jacob shrugged, sipping on his mug of tea. "They may have kept in touch."

"No grandparents," she stated with a note of regret. Grandparents. The idea rolled around in her head. That would be great. She wouldn't be alone anymore. "I wouldn't mind a grandparent or two."

Jacob finished his cup of peppermint tea. "This

is what I'd like to do. I want to start with the agency that placed you with the Grants. They may have some information that we can use. Generally, the agency will ask for a release of information. So it might be a good thing to have you along."

Cynthia nodded. A spark of excitement surged up her spine. Maybe Jacob was the one, the person to help locate her parents. Her thoughts turned to David and her excitement dissipated. David should be with her. He should be the one to help her find her mother, not Jacob. Cynthia wanted and needed David with her. A search like this could strengthen the bonds that drew them together.

"I'm thinking there might be records that we can review. Do you know if your mother was originally from Chicago?"

Shrugging, she answered, "I don't know."

"Do the Daniels know your foster parents? Are they friends?"

"No, they're not friends. Mr. and Mrs. Daniels knew them well enough to call when I stayed over or went on vacation with them. What gave you that impression?"

"You seem so comfortable with them. I thought they might be friends or family and they might have some information that could help our search."

"When I started middle school, Lisa and I became fast friends. As you know, we're still friends today. Miss Helen and Mr. Nick welcomed me into their family. But there wasn't any connection between them and my foster parents."

"And that's how you met David." It was a statement rather than a question.

Cynthia nodded. A smile of remembrance crossed her face, thinking back to the first time Lisa had invited her home. David had been in high school, handsome and strong. He blew Cynthia away; she knew the first time she saw him that this man was for her.

"Are your parents' names listed on your birth certificate?"

"This is the condensed version. Most places accepted this one, so I never needed the full one." Cynthia reached for her purse and removed the wallet-sized sheet. "Here, take a look at it. I don't think it has the info you need."

"Let me see." He reached for the birth certificate and studied it. "It doesn't have much to tell us."

"Well, I was hoping for more info."

"Don't worry about a thing. Look, your birth certificate shows that you were born in Illinois. We'll get a full, certified copy; hopefully, that will give us more to work with."

"I'll do that tomorrow."

"Good." Jacob reached inside his jacket pocket and produced a business card, handing it to Cynthia. "Call me anytime. Have them mail it to my hotel. That way I can work on things when you're not around."

"I intend to see this through. Why wouldn't I be around?"

"You're getting married. There's always planning with that stuff. You may not be available all the time."

Cynthia glanced at the card before stuffing it inside her wallet. There was an edge to his tone when he said "getting married." She examined Jacob, trying to figure out the workings of his mind. *I must be getting too sensitive about this marriage stuff,* she thought, refocusing on the issue at hand.

"Excellent. What I want you to look for is where your mother was born and her full name."

Nodding, she asked, "What about stuff like her Social Security number? Could that help you locate her?"

"Her Social Security number is the most important piece of information we can get. I'll be able to track her on the Internet with that. Then I can tap into the medical database that insurance companies use."

Cynthia's eyes grew large and her voice filled with wonder. "You can do that?"

Chuckling softly, he admitted, "Yeah. Don't spread it around."

"Sweet."

Jacob bowed his head and said, "Thank you. Have you thought about my question?"

"What question?"

"Do you want to meet your mother?"

Her heart sped up before returning to its normal rate. No one, including David, knew how much she wanted to meet her mother. It was a bit of info she kept very deep within.

Cynthia desperately wanted to know why her mother had left her behind. Over the years, she had formed her own story. She had been too young to raise a child alone, or her parents demanded that she give up her baby. Cynthia lifted hopeful eyes to Jacob. "Yes."

"That will be next on our agenda. We'll locate the medical records, then find a current address."

Offering him a tentative but appreciative smile, Cynthia said, "Jacob, thank you. You have no idea how important this is to me."

"No problem," he muttered softly. "I think I understand how you feel."

"But what about your end of the deal?" she asked.

"You mean the apartment?"

"That's it. I need details," Cynthia said, signaling their server.

Jacob smiled. "Such as?"

"House, apartment, or condo? Size? One, two, or three bedrooms? Is there any particular area that you want to live in?"

"I like that lakefront area downtown. It's close to the office and I can ride my bike," he said, switching off the Palm Pilot.

Giggling, Cynthia asked, "You ride a bike?"

"Harley."

"Wow! I'm impressed. So, let's get down to it. How long are you planning to be here?"

"Oh, I need at least a six-month lease. But make sure it's something I can get out of without much fuss."

"I never asked before, but do you have any family? A wife? Kids? Are there certain things you need before I start my search?"

"Couple of bedrooms is my biggest need. There's

no wife or kids, so don't worry about schools or anything like that."

"All right. We're on. How about family?"

"I have parents, but they won't come here, too cold for them. Mom and Dad live in San Diego and they like it there. And so does my sister. She's five years older than me and she's always terrorized me."

Cynthia laughed out loud. "Poor baby."

"I was sometimes. Becky bullied me until I grew taller than her."

She closed her eyes, visualizing how her family would look. "I'd love a family. A brother and maybe a sister." Opening her eyes, she was startled to find Jacob's gaze on her, hot and intense, hunger barely checked blazing back at her. Her breath caught in her throat.

Cynthia blinked and the expression vanished. She studied Jacob's face; nothing remained of the previous emotions. Had she imagined them? She checked her watch and reached for the bill. "Well, it's time for me to get back. I've got a meeting with a vendor in an hour and I need to go over my notes."

"Yeah, it's time," Jacob muttered reluctantly. He plucked the bill from her fingers and studied it.

"Hey," she said, reaching for the check. "This is my treat."

Grinning, he removed several bills from his wallet and tossed them on the table. "No, it's not. This was a working lunch. It's all part of our deal."

Chapter 13

Cynthia and Lisa strolled along Michigan Avenue on a bright summer morning. Their steps slowed, then stopped as they pondered the garments in Lord & Taylor's display window.

Cars zipped by as they resumed their walk. Lisa placed a hand on Cynthia's forearm, halting her at the entrance to Saks Fifth Avenue. They stepped closer to the window, giving other patrons ample room on the crowded street.

Ticking each item on her fingers, Lisa said, "You need a wedding dress and shoes. And that's the basic stuff. How about your trousseau? Since we have the complete day, do you want to look for both our dresses? Speaking of dresses, what do you want me to wear?"

"Time is growing short, we might as well do as much as we can today," Cynthia answered in an even tone. "We're supposed to be in Vegas next weekend. It's time to do the do."

Frowning, Lisa examined Cynthia closely. "Where is the love? You are not acting like a happy, excited bride."

"Sure I am." Cynthia removed her glasses, polishing them on the bottom of her white T-shirt.

"Oh yeah. I can truly see it. Your happiness bubbles over and fills the great outdoors." A burning curious gleam filled Lisa's eyes. She touched her friend's arm. "Sistah girl, what's going on? Come on, tell me the truth."

"What do you mean?" Cynthia was quiet as they walked, as much as she tried to deny it, her last doctor's visit had her terribly shaken. Her jitters about the wedding only added to her despair. Suddenly, she took an intense interest in studying the business suits displayed in the window of Marshall Fields. She sucked the corner of her lip into her mouth while twisting the end of her ponytail around her finger. "Nothing's wrong. Everything's sweet. Perfect."

Exasperated, Lisa sighed. "You know, you are a lousy liar. It's time for you to tell me what's going on. Give."

Without muttering a word, Cynthia moved toward the entrance to Nordstrom's. But Lisa moved faster. She grabbed Cynthia's arm, switched directions, and dragged her into a tiny alcove in the mall. Lisa pushed her buddy onto a bench and sat next to her. Facing her friend, Lisa demanded, "Talk, now."

Cynthia covered her eyes with her hand and answered in a voice that she didn't recognize as her own, "I'm not sure David and I are meant to be together. Maybe we don't have that lifetime kind of love. We're looking at marriage in different ways."

"Cyn! Lifetime kind of love? Of course you

should be together. You and David have loved each other since you were kids. If that's not a lifetime kind of love, I don't know what is."

"I always thought so. Lately we're so far apart on major issues. It's forcing me to rethink us and where we're headed. I'm not sure David and I are ready for marriage and a family."

"It's a little late to try and rethink your life. I mean, you've got a baby to consider."

"Yeah, I know. It doesn't change anything. If I hadn't gotten pregnant, maybe we would have gone our separate ways after a while."

"No." Lisa shook her head and stated firmly, "I don't believe that and you don't either."

"I don't know anymore. Instead of being his wife and life partner, I feel as if David is weighing me as this major asset to his career."

"I don't understand. Explain."

"This wedding. This isn't what I want. It's certainly not how I expected to get married."

"Have you told him this? Why didn't you stop David? Make him understand your feelings? We've talked about our weddings since we were kids. He'll understand."

"I chickened out," Cynthia admitted, feeling heat burn her cheeks.

Lisa sighed, stroking her temples. "I'm probably not the best person to give advice. As you know, I've got personal problems of my own. And I haven't got a clue how to resolve them. But I'm kicking your words back at you. Communication is the key. You have to talk to my brother. He's a man and you have to put your feelings in his face." Lisa took Cynthia's hand and squeezed. "I'll add this and leave the rest alone. If it's not what you want, don't do it. In the end, you'll regret not doing things the way you wanted."

Cynthia held Lisa's gaze with her own. "David is what I want but . . . things are very different from what I expected my life with him to be."

"What do you mean? How different?"

"He wants me to quit my job and stay home with the baby full-time."

Lisa's eyes grew large and she gasped. "What? No way! I mean, you love that job and you're great at it. Talk to Matthew, I'd bet money he'd let you work out something so that you could spend less time in the office as long as you're able to do the job."

"I told David that." Cynthia shrugged. "But it didn't faze him. He kept talking about making partner and how he'll need me to give dinner parties and stuff like that."

"That's not you." With a crinkled brow, Lisa sat quietly observing her friend, then asked, "What else?"

"I really want my own home. I don't want my baby to be raised in a high-rise apartment. Granted, it's a luxury apartment, but it's still an apartment. I want my child to have a backyard in a safe neighborhood. My baby deserves everything that I missed and more. David won't hear of it. He's satisfied with his apartment and that's that. No more discussion."

Lisa began in a soft, caring tone, "Honestly, I can understand the rationale for not buying a house at this point. You two are making some major changes in your lives. Are you sure you want to add the stress of searching for a home on top of the wedding and the baby?"

"Why not? All these things are still going to happen anyway. Why can't we do everything at once and have it all done?"

"I don't know. Why can't you?"

"Because David refuses to bend. I'm lost about how to make him understand."

Standing, Cynthia added an additional item to her growing list of problems. "Plus, it's this Dytech case."

"What about it?" Lisa asked, strolling along beside her buddy.

"It's consuming him. All of his free time and energy are spent working on this case."

"Cyn, isn't that a good thing? I mean, he's trying to make partner."

"That's good on the surface, but at what cost? I don't see him. I don't feel like I can talk to him. Sometimes it feels like I'm marrying a stranger."

"I don't have the right answers for you and my brother. But maybe getting away will help you guys reconnect." Walking back toward Saks, Lisa asked, "By the way, where are we staying in Vegas?"

"The Rio."

"Oh, nice."

Cynthia smiled. "Yeah."

"Tell you what, let's just spend the day together and not worry about our love lives." Lisa stuck out her hand. "Deal?"

"Deal," Cynthia answered, shaking Lisa's hand. "I don't have any set ideas about what you should wear. Let's start here and if something strikes us, we'll get it."

They strolled through the evening dresses department. Lisa picked up a T-strapped gray number. "Pretty."

Cynthia fingered the crepe fabric. "It is. Do you want to try it on?"

Holding the dress against her, Lisa admired the garment in the three-way mirror. "I like it. But it's your wedding. Do you like it? Is it appropriate?"

"We're going to Vegas. Anything goes."

"True." Lisa held Cynthia's gaze with her own. "Okay, I'm going to break my promise. I don't have any answers for you and my brother. All I know for sure is if you don't talk things out, you'll regret it for years to come."

They continued to talk as they sifted through the rack of dresses. "I knew you couldn't keep things to yourself. I know how busy he is and I don't want to add any additional stress to his life right now."

"I understand. Cynthia, it's your wedding and your future. Don't you think you have the right to have things the way you want them?"

"Maybe."

"No maybe."

"Honestly, I feel so guilty about getting pregnant, Lisa. I just keep agreeing to whatever he wants because I feel like I messed up."

"Sistah girl, you need to get over that feeling. You didn't get this way by your lonesome. I'm pretty sure he was right there with you. So stop feeling like you're the culprit. If you had your choice, what would you do for your wedding?"

"I'd like to get married in one of David's judge friends' chambers. With a small reception at your parents' house."

"Suggest that. Explain to him that you'd rather wait a few additional weeks to make your wedding perfect. David's not an ogre. He should understand." Lisa gave Cynthia an encouraging little smile. "He may be a man, but he does listen and try to understand. Just remember, unless you shove things in his face, he'll assume everything is okay."

Cynthia gnawed on her bottom lip, considering Lisa's suggestion. She was tired of the uncertainty and feeling adrift. "Maybe you're right. This is my wedding and my life. I should say something. I mean, what's the worst that could happen? Nothing changes."

Surprised, Lisa stared at her friend. "Good."

"I'm going to finish shopping with you and go by David's place on the way home." Cynthia let out a sigh of relief. She removed a peach silk dress with a slit up the side. "What about this one?"

Lisa reached for the hanger and ran her fingers along the fabric. "It's pretty. I like it. Oh, I love the feel of silk."

"Do you now? I'll have to let Matthew know."

Waving a dismissive hand in Cynthia's direction, Lisa said, "Let's leave Matthew out of the scenario for the moment."

"Can't. He's part of the wedding party, remember?"

Lisa rolled her eyes.

Cynthia watched Lisa sort through another row of dresses. Lisa's face reflected an assortment of conflicting emotions. Fear, pain, and confusion lingered on her delicate features. "Have you decided what you're going to do about him?"

Frowning at her reflection, Lisa shook her head and answered in a tone laced with misery, "I don't know. I just don't know."

"Well, you'd better figure it out before we get to Vegas, if we go to Vegas. Matthew is going to be there with the family. He hasn't pressed you so far, but I have a feeling that's going to change. You know that, don't you? Before David and I get married, you have to get things settled between you and him."

Lisa giggled, shaking her head at her friend. "We're a pair, aren't we?"

Cynthia laughed along with Lisa. "That we are. Hey, I didn't say I had everything together. I'm offering some advice, that's all. Take it or reject it. It's your choice."

Lisa nodded.

"Talk to the man, Lisa. It's time." Cynthia picked up the peach silk and silver crepe dresses and headed to the dressing room. "Come on. These are pretty, why don't you try them on?"

Following the sales assistant to a small cubicle, they crammed into the tiny space and Lisa began to undress. Slipping into the silver dress, Lisa moaned, running an appreciative hand along the neck of the dress. "Oh, I love it." She swirled around in front of the mirrors. "What do you think?"

With her arms folded, Cynthia examined the

dress. "I love it, too. It looks great on you. How do you feel about it?"

"Are you sure this is what you want me to wear? After all, this is *your* wedding."

"I think it's perfect. If we can find some matching shoes and jewelry, the outfit will be perfect. Who knows? You might be too cute for Matthew."

Lisa smirked. "Maybe. Come on, let's pay for this stuff and then it's your turn to search for a dress."

David opened the door dressed in a pair of knee-length gray shorts and a blue Detroit Lions T-shirt. "Hey, Dad. You're a little early."

Holding a milk container full of amber home-made wine, Dad stood on David's doorstep in a pair of overalls, a forest-green short-sleeved shirt, and Nike sneakers. "Yeah, I know. Hope you don't mind."

"No."

"Thanks for having me over. I love watching the game on your big-screen television." Dad cupped a hand near his mouth, lowering his voice to a conspiratorial tone. "If I stick around the house on a Sunday, Helen will create a honey-do list for me to work on."

Chuckling, David took the container from his father's hand. "We can't have that, can we?" That was exactly how his mother operated and he'd seen it all of his life. Once he married Cynthia, he expected to encounter the same treatment. "Dad, you're always welcome. Come on in. We've got a little time before the game starts. I invited J.D. and Eddie. They should be here soon."

He was looking forward to spending some time with his father. Lately, his job had become so consuming he missed game day and dinner with the family.

They both turned and walked down the hallway to the living room. "What's this?" Dad asked, plucking a brown teddy bear that wore a White Sox baseball cap and carried a bat from the copperbrown, leather sofa. "Are you trying to make a fan out of your son before he's born?"

Embarrassed, he recalled walking through the mall and stopping outside the Kay Bee Toy store. The little bear beckoned him and before he knew what happened, he found himself leaving the store with the stuffed animal. "I couldn't resist it. I wanted to buy my baby his first toy," he explained, the heat of being found out filling his cheeks.

"What does Cynthia think of it?" Dad asked, sitting on the sofa.

Standing over his father, David answered, "She hasn't seen it yet. Do you want something to eat?"

"Sure."

"I'll be right back." David lifted the container and added, "I'll take this in the kitchen and put it in the refrigerator." He crossed the mushroom-colored carpeted living room, through the dining room with a cherry-wood table and eight black leather chairs, to the kitchen. In the kitchen, he placed the wine on the island and got glasses from the cabinet. Searching for a tray, he opened the refrigerator and removed a plate of sandwiches.

"Son," his father called.

"Yeah, Dad."

"Do you and Cynthia plan to live here once you get married?"

Returning to the living room with the tray filled with turkey and Swiss cheese sandwiches, David placed the plate on the glass coffee table, added napkins and glasses for drinks. He blew out a hot puff of air and sat in one of the two overstuffed leather chairs. "Cynthia wants a house."

Dad's eyebrows shot up and he probed, "What do you want?"

"I'd like things to be easy. Staying here seems like the right thing to me."

Nodding toward the ceiling-to-floor patio door, Dad said, "That could be a problem for a crawling baby."

David's eyes widened. Fear, hot and real, filled him. He hadn't considered any of that. All he could see was the advantage of staying in his apartment. After all, it was 4,000 square feet with three bedrooms, plus an office. Everything they needed was within walking distance and he didn't have to change his lifestyle or routine.

"Your mother and I stopped by Cynthia's apartment last Saturday. We'd been to the farmers' market and dropped off some fruit and vegetables." Dad broke into his thoughts, stroking his chin and regarding his oldest son carefully.

"Really?" David inquired in a soft tone.

"Mmm-hmm," Dad answered with an eye on the images flashing on the television. "You've been pretty busy lately. What's going on?"

David smiled. "I've been assigned the Dytech case. If I handle things correctly, this one will get me that corner office with the nameplate that reads partner."

As he nodded, Dad's expression stilled and grew serious. "Congratulations. What about Cynthia? How much of your time will this case monopolize and take you away from your family? What's she going to do while you're playing lawyer man?"

Shrugging, David was filled by a feeling of discomfort. "She hasn't said much. But I don't think she's happy with the way things are going. I was hoping she'd want to redecorate this place and work on a nursery."

Dad reached for a sandwich and bit into it. After several minutes, he said, "She admitted to your mother that things aren't perfect between you two and that you guys are working on some stuff. Cynthia talked about her job and your suggestion that she quit it. Why would you want her to do a stupid thing like that?"

Dad's eyes pierced his soul and David felt compelled to defend himself. "I'm doing this for her. Life hasn't always been fair for Cynthia. I want her to have the chance to enjoy an easier life without the stress of worrying about money."

"That's nice. But unrealistic. Money will always be an issue." Dad wiped his mouth with a paper napkin. "Is that what she wants?"

"No."

"Then why are you telling her to do it? Son, Cynthia's smart enough to know what she can and cannot do." Dad picked up his glass and sipped from it. "Don't try to box her in. She's got a mouth and I'm sure she'd tell you if she wanted to stay home after the baby arrives."

"I want to make things easier for all of us." He grew agitated as the enormity of what he was saying registered. His driving need to have his way shocked him. Dad was subtly telling him that he was acting like a tyrant.

"That's commendable." His father reached out and clutched David's arm. "But don't you really mean make life easier for you?"

With a twinge of shame, David's expression became somber.

"You're my son and I know you. You want things simple and uncomplicated. That's not going to happen. There will be two adults in your marriage. Partners. Don't forget it. Cynthia has an equal share in everything that happens in your life. Instead of making decisions and then telling her about them, why don't you ask her what she thinks, sit down, discuss things together, and then come to a mutually agreed upon decision?"

"You're telling me I was wrong."

Dad studied his son for a moment before answering, "Maybe. What I really want to say is don't forget Cynthia's feelings. This is her life too."

"I guess I should think about that."

"Yeah. You should," Dad replied in a matter-of-fact tone.

Smiling, David patted his father's arm. "I promise I will."

The doorbell rang and David hurried to the entrance, eager to see his brothers and enjoy an afternoon of baseball and male bonding. Throughout the afternoon, his father's words lingered in his mind.

Chapter 14

Mustering all of her courage, Cynthia turned the key in the lock, opened the door, and entered the apartment. "David?" she called.

"I'm in the living room, Cyn," he answered.

Her pulse leaped into a gallop. Their relationship had been so crazy, she didn't know what to expect. She did know that they couldn't continue in this limbo land for much longer. She loved him and didn't want to lose him. But Cynthia had reached the point where their relationship needed some boundaries and she didn't plan to leave here until they came to some agreement.

David sat on the sofa in front of the television in a blue-and-white-plaid shirt and jeans. A baseball game was in progress on the screen and his laptop computer was open on the coffee table. His fingers flew across the keyboard as he composed a letter to Simon Broderick. He glanced up and smiled. The warmth of his smile almost made her forget why she was here. Almost.

"Hey," he greeted.

"Hey yourself," she returned.

"What's up?"

"I need to talk to you," Cynthia answered, wetting her dry lips with her tongue.

Surprise flashed across his face before he quickly masked it, offering her a seat with the wave of his hand. "Sure."

Moving across the room, she said, "I've let things eat at me far too long and these things have to be resolved before we get married."

His eyes grew large, but his voice was soft and caring. "What things?"

"Us. Vegas. Our careers. Issues that are troubling me," she explained curtly, twisting her engagement ring around her finger.

He sat very still; his eyes narrowed as he internalized her statement. Like a UAW labor leader negotiating with the auto companies, he said, "Let's start with the biggest issue. Us."

Tipping her head in agreement, she began softly. "I have loved you from the moment Lisa introduced us fourteen years ago. You strolled into your parents' home in your football uniform and I was yours from that moment on." Her voice got stronger as her determination grew. "I loved you then and I love you now, but I won't marry you if you don't bring your attitude about women into the twenty-first century."

He leaned forward and responded in a husky whisper, "And I love you."

"Then why are you acting like a caveman? You man, me woman. A throwback to the Stone Age."

"In my mind, it's my job to protect my family." David ran a hand through his wavy hair. "Be the breadwinner and make sure that you and our baby have everything you need."

A thoughtful smile touched her lips as she formed the right words. "We're both breadwinners. We'll both bring something to the marriage that will help build our home. I don't want a keeper. I need you to be my husband. It's nice that you want to be my protector, but a partner is what I'm looking for."

"I want to be your partner."

"Then stop trying to control me. Honey, saying you love me doesn't put you in charge of my life. This is my life and the only thing you can do is enjoy being with me and come along for the ride." She leaned forward, eager to explain. "Love and marriage are a partnership. Both people, you and me, are equal in that partnership. Bottom line, our decisions have to be made together."

Expressing her feelings to him made Cynthia wonder why she had hesitated. It felt good to get these things off her chest.

"That's what my dad said a while back." His full sensual lips twitched with amusement. "And as usual he was right."

So his family had been talking to him. Good! Validation from a different source always helped.

"Mr. Nick is a very reasonable man," Cynthia said.

"He is. Please listen, I want to explain how my mind's been working."

She inclined her head in compliance. "Okay."

"Sweetheart, your life hasn't always been pleasant. You've gotten some bad deals that weren't your fault. I wanted to make life as beautiful and worry-free as I could. I felt it was my job to take all the stress away and leave you to play and enjoy."

"Thank you for caring. I love that you want to do things for me. But I'm a strong woman and I can handle whatever life hands me. There's a time for play, and when it comes, I want you right there with me. I need you to love me the way I love you. The rest will fall into place with time and care. Let me be your partner." She licked her lips and asked, "Can we agree to talk to each other and not make major decisions without consulting the other person?"

He smiled and inclined his head. "Agreed."

Balling her hands into fists, she muttered, "Yes! This was the right thing to do."

"Let's talk abut Vegas," David suggested. "When you accepted my engagement ring, I asked you if you wanted to have a different type of wedding."

"You did," she conceded. "I should have spoken up. I felt guilty about getting pregnant and I believed I needed to comply with your wishes to offset what I felt was my mistake." She wrinkled her nose. "Inside, I was dying. You and I have talked about what we wanted for our wedding. Vegas isn't it."

"No, it's not," he agreed, touching her hand. "I'd love to have a ceremony that reflected our ideas and beliefs. Unfortunately, time is a factor."

Certain he was talking about the baby, Cynthia said, "The baby isn't an issue. I can wait until we work out the type of wedding we always talked about."

"Actually, it's the Dytech case I'm concerned

with. If we start planning a wedding, it can be interrupted if I have to fly to Philadelphia for depositions or for the trial. Anything can happen, so I don't want to wait."

His reasoning made sense. Still, they could change the plan.

"Originally, I wanted a quick wedding because of the baby." He turned off his laptop and closed it. "Once the Dytech stuff landed on my desk, I realized it was best that we keep to that plan." Standing, he walked to where she sat and stopped in front of her. "Can we compromise on the wedding? Let's stick to the plan. Next week we'll get married in Vegas; then after this case is finished, we'll plan a second wedding like the one we've always dreamed of."

She would have all the fun and excitement of planning her wedding after all. "I can live with that. My job is next on my list."

David's face turned to stone. "This one is going to take some negotiations."

"You are correct about that. My career means as much to me as yours does to you. I've always understood the importance of your work because I feel the same way about mine." Cynthia touched his chest, then hers. "I'm not going to quit my job. I will talk to Matthew about working from home a few days a week. Okay?"

His mouth quirked with humor. "You've made up your mind and it doesn't look as if I can change it. I want you to be happy. If working makes you happy, we'll figure it out."

"Thank you. Now it's time to settle Dytech," she whispered on an ominous note.

"We both know that this case is going to make my career. We'll be in the position to do what we want." He took her hand and kissed it. "Please be patient with me. Ruffino made it impossible for me to reject the case. I promise that I will finish it as quickly as I can so that we can get back to a normal life."

"There are two things that I do understand about you. Your drive and ambition and your need to give your clients 110 percent of your energy and time are major parts of who you are. I want you to be the success that you crave, so I'll bend on this, for now. But I'm reserving the right to revisit this topic at a later date."

David let out a sigh of relief. "Fair enough. Thank you, sweetheart. Have we covered everything?"

"One more thing."

He rose, looking down at her. "I'm sorry I've been so bullheaded. I apologize. More than anything I want us to be happy together."

"I want that too," Cynthia whispered.

"Are we okay now?" he asked, drawing her from the chair.

Nodding, she smiled back at him. "Yes. I think so."

"Good. Can we seal things with a kiss?"

She wrapped her arms around his neck, drawing his face to hers. "That sounds wonderful."

Over his shoulders, her gaze focused on large bag sitting on the sofa. How had she missed it? "What's that?" she asked, pointing.

Turning his head to see what she was talking about, he answered, "That's a present for the baby."

"That's so sweet. Where's mine?"

David pulled her against his chest, taking her lips in a sweet but passionate kiss. Slowly releasing her, he promised, "You get a different present."

Wearing an old pair of jeans, a black T-shirt with Ruffino, Hartman and Black printed on the back and a White Sox baseball cap, David waited for the elevator. He'd completed the final check on his team and now he was ready to leave the office with a clear conscience.

Filled with happiness and anticipation, David exhaled a long sigh of contentment. He and Cynthia had talked and resolved most of their problems. They could go to Vegas and enjoy their wedding without hidden animosity surfacing between them.

The arrival of the elevator pulled him back to the present. The doors opened and Mario Ruffino stepped onto the floor.

"Good." Ruffino's voice boomed as he placed a hand on David's shoulder. "Just the man I wanted to see."

Pointing at the elevator, David said, "I'm on my way out, Mario. Officially, I'm on vacation until late next week. Someone on my team will be happy to help you."

"Vacation." Mario shook his head. "No such thing for a man in your position. Besides, I've got news." He steered him away from the elevator and down the hall.

"Whatever it is, it has to wait," David stated to his boss in a determined, no-nonsense voice. "I'm getting married tomorrow."

"It's going to have to wait," Mario said with cool authority.

"No," David corrected, pushing the older man's hand off his shoulder. "It can't."

Ruffino's white brows formed a straight, intimidating line above his blue eyes. "Let's go to your office and talk."

There was silence between the men until they reached David's office. Once they entered the room, Mario took the guest chair and pointed a finger at the desk, indicating that David should sit behind his desk. He linked his fingers and rested them in his lap, studying David with a steely gleam in his blue eyes. "I need you to go to Philadelphia and head up the team handling Dytech's depositions. The president and chief financial officer will be among the company staff deposed and you should be on hand."

David's pulse shot into orbit. Cynthia would kill him and leave his body for the vultures to finish off if he agreed to this. Given the gravity of the situation, he wouldn't blame her. He needed to reason with Ruffino and reach a compromise.

"Mario, I understand the position you're in. But . . ." David paused, emphasizing the next few words. "I'm getting married Saturday. I can't help you."

Ruffino chuckled nastily. "You're not listening to me. This is your case and you'll be in Philadelphia before the end of the day. You don't have a choice."

He reached inside the breast pocket of his jacket and dropped a business-class ticket on David's desk. "Your plane leaves in three hours. With all the security measures currently in place at the airport, you better hustle if you want to make it on time. A reservation at the downtown Westin Hotel has been made in your name."

Removing a spiral pad from his desk, David jotted down some notes. "I can have Autumn Snyder and Melvin Sullivan fly to Philadelphia. Autumn has been involved since we picked up the case. I'll be on-site before the end of next week."

"You were chosen for this assignment because you promised to do whatever it takes to do the job. Right now, that includes going to Philadelphia. Dytech needs you. I expect you will be on that plane." He stood, straightened his jacket, and said, "You promised complete and total commitment to this case. I expect you to keep your word."

Mario tapped the edge of David's desk, glancing around the room. "Partners at Ruffino, Hartman and Black understand what's expected of them and they do it. They put the company before anything else. If partner is your aspiration, you should remember it."

Was Ruffino threatening him? he wondered. If he wasn't getting married with a baby on the way, he'd quit on the spot. But he had responsibilities now and he couldn't turn his back on that. Plus, this was a bad time to quit a job. The economy hadn't completely rebounded from the recession and few law firms paid as well as this one. Underneath the cover of his desk, David's hands balled into fist. The urge to hit Ruffino was strong. Flexing his hands, he reached for the ticket, hating his boss.

David felt like banging his hand against the desktop. He was completely trapped. Why was this happening to him? This job kept getting in the way of his plans and his family. He had promised Cynthia that he would minimize Dytech's interference in their lives and he'd intended to keep his word.

Picking up the telephone, he dialed Cynthia's work number. Her line was busy and the system immediately switched his call to her voice mail. Hanging up, he drew in a shaky breath and ran a hand through his hair. He didn't want to leave a message because he needed to talk to her, not a machine. She needed the facts from him, personally.

Checking the time, he tried again. For the second time he got transferred to voice mail. Trying her mobile, he got the same treatment. This wasn't his day. What was going on? She always carried her cell with her.

Patting the desk, he decided to wait a few minutes. This was a good time to brief his team, then he'd call again.

Hurrying from the office, he yelled, "Autumn."

She stuck her head in his doorway. "I thought you had left already."

David blew out a hot puff of air and shoved his hands inside the back pockets of his jeans. "Ruffino caught me. I need you to pull the team together ASAP. I've only got a few minutes."

"Got it."

Snatching off his cap, he paced the office. *My life is a mess,* he thought. Returning to his desk, he tried Cynthia a third time. His hands clenched into fists. Voice mail again. "Cynthia, call me on my cell."

Autumn entered with a notepad and pen in her hands. "The rest of the team will be here in a minute. What happened?"

"Ruffino left me with a pile of bad stuff. There's no way out of it. So I've got to fly to Philadelphia."

Her eyelashes flew up. "Ohhh. You're in trouble." Her hand covered her mouth. "What happened?"

"You don't need to know the details," David dismissed, shifting through the files on his desk. "Ruffino made it clear that I have to go. I've been trying to reach Cynthia. She's not answering. Give her a call and let her know what happened. Make sure you tell her that I'll call her after I've checked into the Weston."

"I'd hate to be you right now."

He grunted. "You want to know a secret? I hate being me right now. I've got to go. I've got a window of an hour and a half to pick up my suitcase and head to the airport. My plane leaves at four. Call my folks after you reach Cyn and give them the same info. Here's the work end. Pull all the Dytech data we have. FedEx it to me so that I have something to refer to. Call Olsen and tell him to give me a ring after six."

"This is really bad," she muttered in a broken whisper, clutching her notepad against her chest. "I don't feel comfortable calling your fiancée with news like this, Dave."

Shifting a stack of manila folders under his arm, he touched her arm as he passed her. "I don't want you to have to. I'm going to keep trying to reach her until I get on the plane. I appreciate your help. Thanks, Autumn. I'll be in touch."

Chapter 15

One more day, Cynthia thought, returning to her office. She checked the time and shifted into a faster mode. A surprise bridal shower had taken up two hours of her time and she needed to speed up to get the work on her desk organized. *We'll be in Vegas and I'll be a married woman.*

I have to have everything in order, she thought, checking her to-do list. Since she and David discussed the Vegas wedding, they aimed to stay an extra day or two if time permitted. She wanted her projects ready and available for any member of the team to complete.

Cynthia blew out an unsteady breath of air, fighting the edge of nausea creeping up her throat. Saturday at three she would become Mrs. David Daniels. The enormity of this change in her life made her feel thrilled and fearful at the same time.

She turned to the photos on her desk, searching for reassurance. She smiled, lovingly stroking the framed photo of herself and David when he had graduated from law school. He looked so handsome in his navy blue suit and pastel tie. Her smile slowly disappeared. She'd loved David from the moment Lisa had introduced them, yet she had questioned whether they were on the same page regarding marriage.

Deep in a place that she kept private, Cynthia allowed the image of her ideal wedding to take shape in her mind. There would be a church ceremony with all the members of the Daniels family present, plus her foster parents. Then after several years of marriage and adjusting to all the mundane details, they would make the decision when they planned to have a baby together.

This hurried event with the fewest of family members and friends disturbed her. How could they settle for less when they'd talked extensively about what they wanted at their wedding?

Cynthia glanced out the window, noting a plane flying low. *This time tomorrow I'll be on a plane to Vegas and my whole life will change.* Was she ready for a husband and baby? She hoped so, because once they said I do, their lives were connected forever. Truthfully, they were bound together when they made this baby.

Studying the clock on the wall, she frowned, twisting the ring on her finger. *Where is David? You would think we would have been on the telephone a zillion times discussing the flight to Vegas and our wedding.*

She hadn't heard from him in two days and that was unusual. They always caught up with one another via the telephone before the end of the each day.

She picked up the receiver, ready to call David on his cell phone. Recradling the telephone, she decided against it. David could be in the middle of a case or tying up all loose ends before the weekend.

The phone rang as she returned to her work. *David,* she thought, picking up the receiver. "Good morning, Software Design, this is Cynthia Williams."

There was a palpable pause from the other end. Cynthia could hear a telephone ringing and someone was talking in the background. "Hello? May I help you?"

"Ms. Williams?"

"Yes." The female voice sounded vaguely familiar, but Cynthia had a difficult time placing it.

"This is Autumn Snyder, I'm the legal assistant for David Daniels. We met a couple of weeks ago in his office."

Yeah, she remembered this woman. An image of Autumn wrapped in David's arms made Cynthia's lips curl into an ugly snarl. What did she want? "Yes. What can I do for you?"

"Mr. Williams asked me to give you a call."

Cynthia shot straight up in her chair. Her heart palpitated as her grip on the telephone tightened. *David!* Her voice quivered. "Is Mr. Daniels okay?"

"Ms. Williams, I'm sorry. I didn't mean to frighten you. Mr. Daniels is fine. Just fine."

Cynthia's sigh of relief slithered through the telephone lines. On the heels of her relief another question assaulted her senses. "Then why are you calling me?"

"Mr. Daniels asked me to let you know that he's been called out of town on the law firm's business."

"Out of town? Why?" Cynthia stammered.

Autumn cleared her throat. "The Dytech case is

heating up and he needed to be in Philadelphia to take several depositions."

Good. She had panicked for nothing. "That should be a quick trip. Does he want me to pick him up at the airport? When should I be there? Thursday evening or Friday morning?"

"Umm, Ms. Williams . . ." Amber paused. "I don't believe he'll be returning until late next week."

Stunned, Cynthia shook her head and pulled the phone away from her ear, eyeing the receiver as if it had spouted a string of obscenities. Obviously, this chick had lost her mind.

"Are you telling me that he'll be gone all weekend?" Cynthia asked in a stunned voice.

"Yes, ma'am."

This couldn't be happening. David promised her that his job would not interfere with their plans. How could he renege on their wedding day?

Pain, sharp and powerful, pounded inside her head. She massaged her temple, trying to relieve the tension. This couldn't be happening. Not after all the plans they had made. Not after the promises David had made that nothing would get in the way of them getting married. David insisted that they get married in Vegas so that their wedding wouldn't disturb his court schedule.

All the blood in her body shot to the top of her head. She felt as if she were going to have a stroke. It was a physical battle to push out the next question. "Do you have a number where I can reach him?"

"I have the main number for the Westin Hotel. David's in room 1138. It won't be easy for you to catch him. He's got a pile of depositions to complete before next week."

Cynthia didn't know whether to laugh hysterically or cry. Oh, what the hell! Maybe it was a good thing that they had to wait. David and she seemed to be on opposite ends regarding how their life should proceed.

So we're not getting married this weekend, she mused. But having this woman call added insult to injury. Why hadn't he taken five minutes to call her and make his own apology?

"Ms. Williams? Are you there?"

"Yes." Cynthia drew in a deep breath. She couldn't talk to Autumn a moment longer. "Yes, I'm here. Thank you for calling. I'll let David's family know what's going on. Good-bye."

"Don't you want the—"

Slamming the telephone into the cradle, Cynthia stared out her window, seeing nothing. She willed her mind to go completely blank. As long as she didn't think, the pain that was sure to follow would stay at bay.

What happened to David and me? How could he do me this way? Skip town and leave me with the god-awful task of telling everyone that he wouldn't be available for the wedding? David couldn't have humiliated her more if he'd shouted over the paging system that he didn't want to marry her.

The caliber of the pain between her eyes changed, growing to migraine status. Eventually, Cynthia's emotions overwhelmed her and the tears came. For a while, she gave in to the rush of pain and the feeling of betrayal and, finally, acknowledged that no matter how much she loved David, marriage might not be the correct choice for them.

Afraid someone would barge into her office and see her this way, Cynthia opened her desk drawer and dug inside her purse, searching for a tissue. Her hand touched a crumpled piece of paper. She removed the scrap and smoothed it out.

Well, she could sit here and moan and groan about David, or she could get on with her life. If he had better things to do, so did she. Composing herself, she reached for the telephone. Since David left her with this particular can of worms, she'd make the call to his parents. Mr. and Mrs. Daniels deserved to know what was going on.

Once she finished these calls, she was going to put David Daniels and everything related to him out of her head. She'd concentrate on something important to her and to hell with him. It became very clear that she and David were at the crossroads of their relationship. Now her obligation was to herself and her baby.

Her baby deserved the support of mother, father, and grandparents. She was going on a mission to find her parents so that she and the baby would have the family she never had. Cynthia rubbed a hand over her stomach.

Don't worry; whatever your father does is his business. We're going to get on with our lives and find my mother.

The phone rang more than a half a dozen times before he picked up. "Hello?" Jacob said into the phone.

With her heart in her throat she asked, "Jacob?"

"Yeah." He paused. "Cynthia?"

"Yes. Hi."

"What can I do for you?"

Twisting the telephone cord around her finger, she answered, "You gave me this number a couple of weeks ago and I thought I'd check with you about my birth certificate and what you found."

"Why are you worried about that? Don't you have better things to do, like fly to Vegas and get married?"

"Plan's changed," Cynthia offered by way of explanation.

Jacob's tone was almost too cautious. "Are you telling me you're not getting married?"

"I'm saying I'm not getting married this week." Her voice cracked, but Cynthia quickly recovered. "So let's move on. Have you received a true copy of my birth certificate from the state?"

"Yes. It came in the mail yesterday."

"Why didn't you tell me?"

"You were getting married this weekend, remember? I didn't want to disturb you so close to your wedding."

"Have you found out anything?"

"I'm doing some digging. I've got your mother's and father's full names and I'm trying to match Social Security numbers to the names."

"What's my father's name?"

"Gerald Mason."

She inhaled, surprised. "What happens now?"

"I'll be able to trace where they're working and then you'll be able to visit."

Listening to Jacob, Cynthia felt her pain begin to ease. The hope that she had always tried to control made a grand entrance. "Is there anything I can help you with?"

"Yeah. Since you're not going to Vegas, how about meeting me at your foster parents' house? I'd like to interview them. They may be less reserved if they know I'm working with and for you."

"That'll work. Wouldn't it be better for me to pick you up and we go to their house together?"

"Fair enough. I'm at the Marriott on Michigan. I'll meet you in the drive."

"Give me twenty minutes." She drew in a deep breath. "I'll be there. And, Jacob? Thanks."

Twenty minutes later, Jacob dropped the backpack on the floor in front of him, snapped his seat belt into place, and turned to face Cynthia. He smiled at her and said, "I thought we'd go by the agency first. See what we can find out from them, then visit your foster parents if you think that would be okay."

"Fine," Cynthia answered, shifting into drive. "Once we're done, do you want to look at some apartments? Have you thought about a town house? That would give you more space."

"Are you sure you don't have any other commitments? I don't want to take up too much of your time."

"There isn't any trouble. Besides, you're helping me. Our deal was that I would help you find a place to live."

"Yeah, but . . ." He hesitated, taking a long hard look at her. "You had big plans for this weekend. Maybe something can change."

Suddenly the car became too small; she felt warm all over. "No. It won't. David's out of town. So let's get on with our business."

Unzipping his backpack, Jacob pulled a Palm Pilot from it and switched it on. "Works for me."

Chapter 16

"Ta da," Helen sang, displaying a two-tiered wedding cake. She placed her creation on the coffee table and turned to her family. This was a joyful time for everyone. All of her children were here to support their big brother's marriage.

"Oh, Ma. It's beautiful!" Jenn praised. "Did you make it?"

"Yes, I did."

Jenn predicted, "David and Cyn are going to be so surprised!"

"Thank you." Smiling, Helen admired her handiwork and said, "I hope they will. I wanted to do something special for them since they're not going to have a traditional wedding."

Taking her daughter-in-law's hands, Helen asked, "Jenn, how are you doing? I've been so busy I haven't had a minute to talk with you. Are you feeling okay?"

"I'm fine. The baby, Eddie, and I are doing really well." Jenn rubbed her belly.

"Good."

J.D. wrapped an arm around his mother and hugged her. "You are the best. This is thoughtful."

"Thank you, my second son. Have you guys got all the luggage in the van?" Helen glanced from one son to the other.

Laughing, Eddie nodded. "Go take a peek at Dad. He's got the baggage organized just so. You'd think we're planning to be away for a month instead of a long weekend. Suitcases are stacked to the roof of the van. I'm not sure there's enough room for us to get to the airport. I sincerely hope the happy couple plans to drive their own car."

Helen waved away his concern. "We'll worry about seating when the marrying folks arrive. As long as everyone is here and we're ready, that's all I'm concerned with. Lisa, come help me with the champagne and glasses."

"Okay."

"Honey, when will Matthew get here?" Helen asked, watching her daughter very closely.

"He'll meet us in Vegas later this evening. There's a couple of things he needed to finish before he could leave town."

Not completely satisfied with Lisa's answer, Helen nodded, holding her tongue. Once things settled down after the wedding, they'd have a chance to explore the topic of Matthew and Lisa's relationship.

Lisa's forehead wrinkled after glancing at the clock on the white microwave. She asked in a worried tone, "Ma, what time did David say they would be here? It's getting late."

"You're right. I'm a bit concerned." She handed the bottle of champagne to Lisa and pointed to the wineglasses. "Don't forget napkins. Thanks, hon."

The phone rang as she reached for it to call David. "Let me get this, then I'll call your brother."

Freddie Jackson's "You Are My Lady," filled the room from the home entertainment center. J.D. relaxed on the sofa, watching *Buffy the Vampire Slayer* reruns, while Jenn and Eddie furiously tried to hide their wedding gift in Jenn's carry-on luggage. In the opposite corner of the room, Lisa and Vee conversed in quiet tones.

Helen moved swiftly into the room and switched off the CD player. "Well, you can unpack the van," she announced in a tone that was one step away from rage. "The wedding's off!"

"What! How!" Jumping to her feet, Lisa hurried across the room and stood next to her mother.

"Oh no!' Jenn cried. Smoothing her top over the swell of her stomach, she shook her head. "Those two are having such a difficult time."

"The wedding's off?" J.D. moved around the coffee table to stand near his mother. "Why? What happened? How's Cynthia? Where's David?"

"All very good questions," Helen said. She folded her arms across her chest. "I just spoke with your brother's law clerk, Autumn Snyder. David asked her to call us because he's on a plane to Philadelphia that left at four o'clock.

Scrunching up her face, Vee asked, "Philadelphia? What's in Philadelphia?" Nick strolled into the room and answered in a confident voice, "It's that Dytech case, isn't it?"

Helen nodded.

"I told that man that the case would come between him and his family. And I'm sorry to say that

I'm right." He moaned sorrowfully. "This is not good."

"I don't know where my brother keeps his brains." J.D. shut his eyes and shook his head. "Obviously, they're not where they should be." Tossing his hands in the air, he said to no one in particular, "How could he do this to Cynthia? She's a great woman and she definitely deserves much better. Has anybody talked to her?"

Patting J.D.'s hand, Helen strolled across the room and picked up the cordless phone. "I'll call her now. She needs her family. I don't want her to be alone. Maybe I can convince her to come and stay with us for a few days."

"That's a good idea, Helen," Nick said.

"No answer. She's not at work or home." Helen disconnected the call and returned the phone to its cradle. "I never believed a son of mine could be this callous."

"Maybe we should pile in the van and go to Cyn's place and see about her." Lisa touched her mother's hand.

"Yeah, that's a great idea," Nick concurred. "Let's go."

The Danielses hurried from the room to the van.

Three hours later, the family returned to the house exhausted and frustrated. Helen marched into the family room and picked up the phone. She tried Cynthia's number again but got her answering machine.

"I don't know what to do," Helen admitted, tossing her hands in the air.

Lisa wrapped an arm around her shoulders and suggested, "Maybe she wants to be alone. I mean, this is so humiliating."

"I know. I just don't understand what's going on with your brother. But I want to help Cynthia." Helen brushed away a tear.

"Ma, we have to respect her feelings. I'll try her tomorrow morning."

"Thanks, hon. I want her to know that we're here for her."

Chapter 17

Dressed in a faded T-shirt with x-men plastered on the front, Jacob strolled across Shaw's Crab House with his hands stuffed inside the back pockets of his jeans. Matthew chuckled. His buddy didn't care about clothes, or much else, unless it involved computers or work.

He stopped at the table. Matthew rose and greeted Jacob with an outstretched hand. "Hey, man. It's good to see you."

"You, too." Jacob pulled out the chair opposite Matthew and slipped into it. "What's up?"

"I thought you might enjoy getting out of the hotel." Returning to his chair, Matthew shook out a white linen napkin and draped it across his lap. "You know, have dinner in a nice restaurant and chew the fat."

Jacob grinned back at him. "I'm all for a free meal, especially at my boss's expense. Besides, I'm tired of eating by myself."

"That's not what I hear," Matthew stated with an upward sweep of his brow. "I understand you and Ms. Williams were out and about a few days ago."

For half a second, Jacob's expression remained

passive. Red color flooded his cheeks and the tips of his ears. Jacob looked as if he'd been caught swimming nude on a public beach. "That's interesting," he said in a calm, almost too casual tone. "Where did you get that bit of info? And when did you start listening to gossip?"

"Don't," Matthew stated with a negative shake of his head. "I saw you two pull off in Cynthia's car."

Nodding, Jacob turned to the waiter hovering at his side. "Let me get a triple shot of Martell, no ice." With a quiet, efficient air, the waiter turned to Matthew, pad and pen at the ready.

Matthew scratched the side of his neck with a single finger. Things needed to be discussed and he wanted to be clear when he talked to Jacob. "Make mine a bit milder. Shot of Johnny Walker, plenty of ice."

The waiter distributed menus, read the specials from his pad, and dutifully left the pair to their conversation. Silently, Matthew and Jacob considered their choices for dinner. They ordered when the waiter returned with their drinks. Jacob sipped on his Martell for several moments before asking, "Did you invite me here to discuss Cynthia and me?"

Matthew's hand circled his glass. "No. Cynthia's not my prime reason. It's been a while since we've touched base. I want to know what's going on with you, that's all."

The waiter returned, delivering a basket of freshly baked rolls and two orders of shrimp cocktail. Lifting the napkin away from the rolls, Matthew sniffed appreciatively as the aroma of warm butter and garlic tickled his nose.

"Fair enough. Let's talk business. I traced several of Stephen's buyers." Jacob sipped his drink. "Do you want me to approach them?"

"No. Give me the info." He swirled a shrimp into the cocktail sauce and bit into it. "I'll contact them and give them a chance before turning the info over to the police."

"No problem."

An uncomfortable silence followed. Matthew wanted to talk about Cynthia to give Jacob a piece of advice that might save his heart. But he faltered over how to approach his buddy without creating a rift between them. The problem was taken out out of his hands.

"Cynthia and I have an agreement," Jacob explained, before popping a corner of a roll into his mouth. "I'm helping her with a personal project and she's going to help me find a place to live since I don't know how long I'll be staying in Chicago and you haven't given me a date for your wedding."

Matthew ignored the hint. Instead, he raised his hand in an act of surrender.

"How's that working out for you?"

Eyeing Matthew from under lowered lashes, Jacob explained, "We checked out a couple of apartments. Saw some nice stuff downtown."

"You don't have to tell me anything. This is your business, not mine."

He chuckled. "Actually, it's your business, too. After all, Cynthia works for you. She's your fiancée's best friend and engaged to her brother. I'd say you have a vested interest in this situation and its outcome."

"Is there a situation?"

"Not really," Jacob answered.

"I mean . . ." Matthew stopped, selecting his words with great care. "You just got out of a situation with your girlfriend. Are you ready to put your emotions on the line so soon?"

Shaking his head, Jacob replied, "My heart's not on the line."

Matthew put down his fork and studied Jacob. After a moment he said, "You've got that look."

"What look?"

Matthew sipped from his glass. "The one that signals that you're interested and says you want to see where this thing leads you. Let me tell you where you're going: it's down a bumpy, hazardous, pit-filled road. Don't forget the lady is engaged, plus pregnant."

"I haven't forgotten any of that. Don't worry. I'm not putting myself on the line." A steely edge entered Jacob's voice at the same time his eyes flashed a warning.

"Jay, you're my friend and I don't want to see you get hurt. Are you sure you know what you're doing?"

"Mattie, there's nothing to worry about. Cynthia and I are friends. Nothing more."

Matthew drew in a deep breath and let it out slowly, strumming his fingers against the linen-covered tabletop. "This is not a conversation I'd normally have. You're a big boy and I assume you know what you're doing. Let me remind you, before we caught Stephen with his hand in my pocket, you'd expressed some interest in Cynthia. I admit things are shaky between Cynthia and David and it's a great opportunity to pick up the pieces if things don't pan out between them. But are you sure you're doing the right thing?"

Jacob busied himself buttering a roll while a slow, easy smile stretched across his tan skin. "Stop worrying. You're taking this way too seriously. Yeah, I like the woman. And she's going through a rough time right now. I'm not going to take advantage and my heart is safe. Things are okay. We're helping each other."

Running a hand over his face, Matthew advised, "Brother man, you are lying to yourself. Things are far from okay. I'm going to take you back to some advice you gave me. Remember what you told me? Don't fall. I'm handing those words back to you."

"I don't need them. It's not a problem."

"Famous last words. I think I might have said something along those lines myself. And, honestly, I was too enthralled to see anything but Lisa." Matthew chuckled, settling more comfortably in his chair. "You're my friend and I care about what happens to you. If you're not careful, you're going to be the one hurting."

Jacob began to laugh. The sound grew louder, carrying across the room. Several patrons glanced their way, evaluating the situation. When they found nothing interesting, they returned to their meals.

Matthew asked, "What in the hell are you laughing at?"

"I love how you are trying to offer advice when you didn't take it when it was given to you. If you recall, you did fall and hard. So hard that you now are going to marry the woman. When did you become an authority?"

"Okay, smart-ass. I'm trying to help you out here. Once David gets back to Chicago and pleads his case, all will be forgiven. Cynthia and David will set a new date and he'll make sure he makes it to Vegas the second time."

"What happens if she decides not to forgive him? He may have blown it for good."

"Never happen." Matthew spoke with confidence. "Lisa's always telling me how much Cynthia loves David, has loved him since they were children. Plus, there's a baby involved. She'll do the right thing for herself and her baby."

The arrival of their dinner cut the conversation short. Matthew leaned heavily into his chair as the waiter placed grilled sea bass, garlic mashed potatoes, and a vegetable medley of summer squash, asparagus, and carrots in front of him.

Jacob grimaced and Matthew knew he'd hit a nerve. Matthew wished Jacob would find someone that could appreciate him. Cynthia wasn't the woman for him. From everything Lisa had told him about David and Cynthia's relationship, Cynthia would forgive David. Time would settle everything. It was best for Jacob to pull himself together and stop acting like a lovesick puppy.

"What about Lisa?" Jay fired back. "What's going on there? I haven't heard you say anything about your wedding in weeks."

Matthew felt the rush of heat paint his cheeks a faint shade of red. Now the hot seat belonged to him. The meal, arranged so appealing on the plate, turned to trash before Matthew's eyes. Lisa refused to discuss their wedding. Lately, she avoided spending time with him.

He tipped his head in silent acknowledgment of Jacob's direct hit. "You've got me. It's obvious that I didn't take your advice and I'm paying for it now."

Remorse replaced the smug expression of triumph on Jay's face. "I'm sorry, man. You hit me hard and I came back fighting."

With a self-mocking shrug, Matthew admitted, "You're right. Who am I to tell you a thing? I can't take care of my own business."

"What's happening?"

"Since Cynthia announced the pregnancy thing, Lisa has shut down on me. She won't discuss the wedding or anything related to our lives together. Honestly, I expect her to return my ring any day."

"No, man. Lisa loves you. I know she does."

"You're right, she does. But having a baby is so damn important to her." He ran a hand over his face. "I don't know how to help her accept it. Before Cynthia got pregnant, Lisa would discuss the possibility of adopting. Now if I mention the word, she freezes up, then changes the subject. I don't know what to do."

"What about counseling? Do you think that might help?" Jacob finished his drink and signaled the waiter for a second.

"I'm willing. But I don't think Lisa will agree."

"Why not?"

She's too fragile. Right now, the slightest nudge

might take her over the edge. I won't do that to her."

"Here's your reality check. If she's that close to the edge, something's going to take her over the edge. You better be ready for it."

Matthew ran his hand over his head. Jay was right. Lisa was ready to explode and anything might set her off. Maybe it was time to talk to her parents; let them in on things and discuss their options. "I know you're right. I'm thinking I might talk to Mr. and Mrs. Daniels."

Pointing a finger at Matthew, Jacob said, "Good idea. If they're involved, you've got some help and maybe a little insight into what's going on inside your girl's brain."

"That's the problem. She's not happy with the cards life dealt her and she's trying to get around them. Sometimes you have to accept life the way it is and get on with it."

"Keep in mind this route could be tricky. Lisa might resent your getting her family involved in her business. How will you get out of that one?"

Weariness drained Matthew. He didn't know how to handle it. He found this relationship stuff more difficult than running a company. "I don't know."

"My advice: don't do anything until you've figured it all out. Put every piece in place. Don't leave anything to chance if you can help it."

Nodding, Matthew muttered, "You're right. Damn, I love that woman and I want her to be happy with me and with herself. Why can't she accept what life has given her?"

"Do any of us?"

Chuckling, Matthew answered, "No. I've seen Lisa's big close-knit family for myself. We may never have the same thing, but she understands what it's like and I'm not sure she can handle the difference."

"Most times we try to rearrange things so that they better suit what we have in mind for our lives."

Matthew stared hard at Jacob. There was a note in his friend's voice that made Matthew think that he was talking about himself and Cynthia. Was he trying to even the odds against David, so that he had a better shot at Cynthia? Could be. Matthew suspected Jacob was headed down a hard road.

Chapter 18

David slid the key card into the slot and opened his hotel room door. He stepped inside, shut the door behind him, and crossed the spacious living area to the bedroom. Ignoring the elegant oak bedroom furnishings, he tossed the plastic entry card on the dresser and crossed the room.

"Man, I'm tired," he muttered, working his shoulders to relieve some of the tension. The attorneys for the plaintiffs were tough and he expected to face stronger opposition as the depositions continued.

David turned to the desk, expecting to see the blinking red light on the telephone console. Disappointed, he opened the refrigerator door, removed a miniature bottle of scotch, and tossed several ice cubes into the bottom of a glass. Taking the glass and the bottle with him, he dropped onto the bed covered by a striped silver and white comforter and tossed the tube-shaped white pillow on the opposite side of his king-size bed.

He rubbed his forehead, trying to relieve the dull ache pushing to the front of his head. Cynthia hadn't called. Did that mean she was still upset with him, or had she forgiven him for the last-minute change of plans? He hoped so. He needed to talk with her, make his apologies, and try to explain how he got stuck in the middle of this Ruffino muck-up.

Cynthia had always understood his ambition and the importance of this particular case. In the past, she had stood firmly in his corner and behind the things he was trying to accomplish. But this was different, his conscience reminded him. He'd practically left her standing at the altar. This was his bad. Really bad. But things couldn't be helped, he thought. Cynthia would understand that. She always did. Once he explained the situation and made his apologies, they could set a new date.

Mentally rehearsing his explanation, David dialed her home number. *Ruffino caught me on the way out. I was at the elevator and the doors opened and the old man stepped out. What could I do? I was trapped. I had no idea that I would be called away like this.*

"Damn answering machine," he muttered, slamming the phone down without savoring the seductive tone of Cynthia's voice on the machine. He didn't want to talk with her voice mail; he wanted to talk with Cynthia. Maybe he should have left a message with the hotel number on it for her to call or try to explain on the machine? He opted out of leaving a message. This topic needed to be addressed one on one.

David glanced at his watch. It was after seven; she should be home by now. Where in the heck was she?

He punched in Cynthia's cell phone number,

certain she'd pick up. There was no way she'd leave home without her mobile phone. Again her voice mail kicked in and he hung up. *Where is she?* he wondered, swallowing the last drops of scotch.

Standing, David loosened his tie, removed his jacket, and headed for the bathroom. The telephone began to ring and he rushed across the bed. Had she used caller ID and realized it was him?

"Hello?" he breathed into the phone in a hurried whisper, sinking into the soft mattress.

"Umm. David?"

Autumn. Disappointment spread through him like unpleasant gossip through a neighborhood. Frustrated and disappointed, he mumbled, "Hey. What's going on?"

"Nothing. I wanted to check on you and see how the deps went."

"Good, so far," he answered, stretching out on the bed.

"Glad to hear it. I wanted to know if you needed anything from me or the office. It's quiet here without you and I felt I should check to see if there's any research you need me to do."

"I can't think of anything," he answered, scratching the side of his neck. "At least, not yet. I'll probably get the transcript back later this week. There's a minimum of thirty additional employees to depose. I'll be here at least four or five more days."

"Thirty people. Wow!"

Chuckling, he said, "That sums things up."

"You're all set then?" she asked.

"For now. When I get to some of the top execs, I

might need you to pull old transcripts from previous records so that I can compare them. Right now, things are going pretty smooth."

"Good. Have some fun while you're in Philadelphia and I'll give you a call tomorrow. Bye."

"Umm!" David threw his legs over the side of the bed and sat up. Tension knotted his shoulders again and he rolled them. "Hey, Autumn."

"Yeah?"

"Were you able to get in touch with Cynthia?"

"Oh. I'm sorry. I forgot to mention it. Yes, I reached her at her office."

"Good." He swallowed hard. "How did she take the news?"

Silence followed. Autumn's disapproval reached through the phone line, wrapped its hands around his throat, and almost strangled him. His lips pursed, then he said in a resigned voice, "Give it to me straight. I need to know if the news upset her."

"Ms. Williams didn't seem upset. At first she thought that something had happened to you. That you might have been in an accident or something. Once I assured her that you were fine, she took the news well. She was quiet for a minute, then she thanked me and hung up."

"Did you give her the hotel's number and my room number?"

"Yes."

"Who did you call first, my parents or Cynthia?"

"Ms. Williams. She also said that she would get in touch with your parents."

Frustrated, David ran a hand over his face. So far, nothing Autumn had said gave him a clue regarding Cynthia's feelings. Was she fighting mad, ready to kill him, or did she truly understand and want him to return to Chicago so that they could reschedule their trip to Vegas?

"So she seemed okay? Not upset?"

"To be perfectly honest, I really expected her to explode, hear fireworks. But she didn't raise her voice."

"Did Cynthia say what she planned to do next? I mean, I know she called my folks, then what? What about after that? Did she say whether she planned to head home or maybe go to my sister's?"

"I'm sorry. She didn't say."

"I'll try her again after I get something to eat." He removed his tie and unbuttoned his shirt. "In the meantime, send six dozen long-stemmed roses to her place with a note from me. Just say, I'm sorry on each card. I'll smooth things over when I reach her."

"Mmm."

"What?" David asked, hearing something unpleasant in Autumn's tone.

"Are you sure flowers are enough?"

"What do you mean?"

"I'd be fighting mad if you'd stood me up, left me at the altar," she amended. "You'd have to grovel a bit more. In addition to flowers, I'd need many, many presents before you got back into my good graces."

"It's fortunate that I'm not engaged to you."

"Hey, make fun of me if you want. You're the one in trouble."

"Generally, Cynthia understands about my job.

She knows that I don't always have control over what happens. It'll be okay."

"I really hope you're right. But if I were you, I'd be ready to produce jewelry, a pound of platinum, something very special to help smooth over the rough spots. You're going to need them."

"If I'm wrong, when I get back to Chicago I'll take whatever punishment she dishes."

"David," Autumn said, then stopped.

"Yeah?"

"Nothing."

"Come on. Don't stop now. If you have something to add, now is the time."

"All right, I will. Ms. Williams understands, but there will be a point where she'll get sick of being put second to your career. Think about it."

David's arm rose and flopped on the bed at his side. Nobody understood their relationship. "Thank you. I'll take it under advisement," he said. Autumn could be right, but he needed to talk to Cynthia so that he knew how upset she felt before he did anything. "If I'm going to apologize the flowers should do it."

"Dream on. You'll probably get a big surprise."

"You may think you know, but my girl understands. She'll be fine."

"I think you've been taking that woman's good heart for granted," Autumn added carefully as she remembered she was talking to her boss.

"For granted? You're mistaken."

"Maybe so. I'll call tomorrow evening to see if there is anything you need help with. Good night."

"Good night," David muttered, dropping the

telephone back into the cradle and stretching out on the bed. *Taking Cyn for granted. I don't think so,* he dismissed.

David needed a shower, a change of clothes, and some food before he tackled anything else. Heading for the bathroom, he removed his shirt and tossed it on the bed.

Running his shower, he added a touch of cold water and stepped out of his remaining clothes. The water felt good against his skin, and for a few minutes he let the cares of the day run down the drain with the water.

Lathering his body, he considered Autumn's comment. Had he done more damage than he believed possible? Granted, leaving town without a call had not been a good thing for his relationship with Cynthia. But, like most bad things, they always happened at the most inopportune time. Plus, he hadn't had any choice in the matter. When Ruffino said, "go," you went.

The old man had given him a plane ticket and an itinerary for the depositions and told him to leave right then. He stopped by his place to pack a bag and went on to the airport. Each time he'd called Cyn's office, he got her voice mail.

Cynthia deserved more than a Dear John telephone call from your assistant, his conscience admonished him. *You flew off without calling her. That was wrong, attorney Dave. She's always been in your corner, no matter what.*

That thought tore at his insides. Cynthia had admitted feeling uncertain about the whole getting married stuff and here he was in another city. *I need to talk to her now,* he decided, turning off the water, stepping from the shower, and doing a quick dry-off. He wrapped a towel around his middle and made his way back to the phone determined to tell her how much she meant to him.

David sat on the edge of his bed and dialed Cynthia's number. The telephone rang four times before she answered.

"Hello?" she said into the phone.

"Hey, babe," he began, floundering over what to say next.

"Hello, David."

The words rushed from him. "Cyn, I don't know what to say. Yes, I do. I'm sorry. Ruffino caught me as I was leaving the office and he demanded that I fly to Philadelphia. I'm sorry, baby. I'm sorry."

"Mmm-hmm."

"What does that mean? You're probably angry and I understand. But I promise I'll make this up to you. Truly."

"Mmm-hmm."

"I love you and I want us to get married as soon as I get back, even if we have to fly to Vegas without the family. You and the baby are my priority."

An uncomfortable silence settled between them. This silence unnerved him in a way that he couldn't explain.

"Are you all right, Cyn?"

"Yes."

That one-word answer told him nothing. At this

point, he didn't have a clue if she understood what he was saying or not.

"I called earlier, but I didn't get an answer. I even tried your cell phone. Where were you, babe? You always pick up your cell."

"I . . . um, um, left it at home."

"Home?"

"Yes. I didn't bring it with me because I figured I wouldn't need it."

"Where did you go after you left work? I called your apartment. You weren't home."

"I needed time to think."

"But where did you go?"

"Out."

"Cyn—"

"David, there's someone at my door. We'll talk when you get home. Bye."

Before he uttered another word she hung up. Uneasiness crept into his heart. What was going on?

He sat holding the telephone as a feeling of discontent flooded his veins. Had he made things worse with this call? Cynthia seemed aloof in a way that he'd never encountered and he didn't know how to handle those feelings or her. Hopefully, by the time he returned to Chicago, she'd calm down and allow him to explain. Then they could choose a new day for their wedding. If there would still be one.

Chapter 19

Lisa parked in Matthew's circular drive and rested her head against the steering wheel as a chill seeped into her soul. All she truly wanted to do was rush inside and stay with Matthew forever. But that wasn't possible. She lifted her head and left the car, searching for the strength to do what she must.

Admiring Matthew's house from the driveway, she experienced a surge of regret and longing sweeping through her, making her feel old and battered. She'd loved this house from the moment she and Matthew had found it.

Their plans for the future lingered in her thoughts, causing pain to replace regret. She was ending their relationship for Matthew's good, for his future, to save him from a life without his own children.

She swallowed the lump in her throat and moved around the car. With achingly slow movements, she climbed the steps and rang the doorbell. Her heart pounded so fast in her chest it felt as if she might have a heart attack on the spot.

She blew out a hot puff of air, waiting. Seconds later, Matthew opened the door.

"Hi," he greeted, smiling broadly before asking in a gentle, soft voice, "What brings you out tonight?"

Looking into Matthew's earnest face, Lisa responded to the welcome in his smile. *I can't do this,* she cried silently. *I love him too much.* She pressed a smile onto her lips and answered, "I finished at the office and wanted to spend a little time with you. Is that okay?"

He drew her into the house with a hand at her waist. "Lee, you are always welcome. Besides, once we're married, this will be your home. To be perfectly honest, I've missed you."

Swallowing hard, she asked, "What are you up to?"

"I was upstairs in the bedroom listening to some music. Come on." He took her hand and hurried across the foyer to the staircase. "I've got Boney James's latest CD on the player."

She held back. Her steps slowed as her mind burned with the memories of the times she had shared in that room with him.

Her heart hammered foolishly in her chest as they drew near the den. The smooth sounds of Boney James's saxophone reached them before they entered the room. Matthew guided her to the sofa with a warm hand planted firmly on her waist.

After getting her comfortable, he sat next to her. "I'm glad you came. It's been way too long since we've had time together." His fingers sensuously slid a tendril of hair behind her ear. "I've missed you."

Lisa offered him a nervous smile. "And I've

missed you." Once those words were out of her mouth, she realized how true they were. For several weeks, avoiding Matthew had been her full-time job. It was a job she hated.

He took her hand and lifted it to his lips. The touch of his lips made her heart flutter.

Wrapping a hand around her waist, he drew her form to him. Her heart raced as Matthew's moist breath fanned her face. Lisa sank into his cushioned embrace. His lips claimed hers in a slow, thorough kiss.

Coming up for air, they parted reluctantly.

"We really need to talk," Matthew whispered into her hair.

"We should."

He brushed a gentle series of kisses across her forehead and down her cheek, then recaptured her lips in a drugging kiss. Surrendering to his hungry mouth, Lisa forgot her plan and concentrated on responding to the demands of his lips. She'd deal with the other stuff later.

He swung her into the circle of his arms and strolled across the room, stopping next to the bed. Raining tiny kisses on her lips, he said, "I know things haven't been good between us lately. But we'll get through this. Your coming here tells me that you want things to work out as much as I do."

Lisa found herself in the center of the mattress with Matthew at her side. "I-I-I," she stammered, feeling completely guilty.

Matthew hushed her with another kiss. "No. Let me finish. I've never denied that I wanted children.

I love you." His lips brushed against her lips as he spoke. "But I want you more."

Every word he uttered filled her with hope. She wanted to believe him, but she knew nothing had changed between them.

Resting her head against his chest, she said, "Your words are so perfect that I almost believe you. How are you going to feel ten years from now? Or when you're ready to retire and there's no one to leave your company to?"

"I can't worry about what-ifs. You are the most important thing to me." Matthew cupped her cheek, punctuating that statement with a kiss that shattered her calm and communicated his hunger for her.

His hands were everywhere. His fingers outlined the swell of her breast, moving inward to draw a circle around her nipple. Lisa pressed her lips against the smooth column of his throat, feeling his pulse accelerate.

"Wait." She tasted his skin, enjoying the rough feel of him as she teased him with tiny kisses down his chest. "Let me."

Wet kisses left a trail from his breast to his navel. She unsnapped, unzipped, and dragged his jeans off his body, freeing his flesh from its confines. He sprang full, pulsating and erect. Lisa caressed him gently, feeling his flesh quiver under her touch.

Her breath caught in her throat as his hands roamed intimately over her breasts. Lisa's eyes drifted shut, enjoying the feel of his hands on her flesh. Each stroke of his fingers sent pleasure jolts through her. She didn't want him to stop. Aroused, she drew herself closer to him, moaning softly. It had been weeks since they'd last made love and she wanted to feel him inside her.

Turning her attention to his broad chest, she stroked his flesh through the cotton fabric. With heady delight she watched as his nipples became erect. For their last time together, she'd give him a wonderful good-bye. Lisa wanted to do something special for him. Offer him a part of herself no one else had ever experienced and he'd always remember.

Lisa helped him out of his T-shirt, marveling at how well toned his shoulders and chest felt under her eager hands. Her tongue flicked out and licked his nipples, outlining the dark circles before drawing one into her mouth. She made a wet path down his ribs to his stomach and halted to worship his navel for a second before moving lower. Matthew's breath became ragged and shallow, but he made no moves to stop her.

Lisa positioned herself between his spread legs as she caressed and stroked his throbbing erection.

"Lee!" Matthew groaned, running trembling fingers through her hair. "Do you know what you're doing?"

Lisa wasn't certain. She'd never done this before, but she planned to love him as completely as she knew how. Her hands stroked up the side of his manhood and she followed that gesture with her tongue. Inch by tantalizing inch, she learned the unique taste and texture of Matthew. He felt smooth and hard, all at the same time. She circled the tip of his flesh with her tongue, then sucked gently on the top.

For a second, it seemed that Matthew had stopped breathing, then he gasped. His hips rose off the bed while his flesh filled her mouth. Lisa held firm, loving him with her tongue.

Her tongue licked the first drop that seeped from his flesh. Matthew's fingers were entwined in her hair, forcing her to release him. Raising her quickly up the length of his body, he captured her lips in a fierce kiss. "I love you, Lee," he breathed into her mouth.

Matthew rolled over, grabbing a condom from the nightstand before positioning Lisa beneath him and sinking into her welcome sheath. Lisa clung to him, wrapping her legs around his waist, arching her back to meet his gentle stroking. He rocked his hips, withdrawing slightly and thrusting inside her again and again, setting a slow pace that fanned the fires smoldering inside her.

Lisa rose, meeting each thrust with uncontrolled passion. His rhythm bound her in coils of increasing pleasure and she gasped in sweet agony. Her cries of pleasure mounted to a pinnacle. The first tremor hit her like an avalanche, showering her world with ecstasy. Seconds later, his moan of release punctured the air and they floated back to earth together.

Hours later, Lisa drifted from her euphoric haze. Wrapped securely in Matthew's arm, she stroked his limb, snuggling deeper into his warm cocoon.

She hated to leave him, wanted more than anything to remain safe and secure within his embrace, but that wasn't possible.

Lisa slipped silently from the bed and picked up her dress from the floor. Matthew's regular breathing let her know that he was still deeply asleep. Shutting her eyes, she prayed for the strength to leave him.

She stepped into her sundress, adjusting the straps over her shoulders. Barefoot, she moved across the room and plucked her purse and shoes from the sofa.

This was far more difficult than she'd imagined. Ending her engagement, leaving Matthew. Never seeing him again hurt so much that she felt the pain as if someone had stuck a knife through her heart.

For a moment, she stood next to the bed, watching Matthew, memorizing each line and curve of his face. *I will always love you,* she promised silently. Fighting back tears, Lisa pulled the ring from her finger and placed it on the table next to the bed. Touching two fingers to her lips, she gently touched Matthew's mouth. She opened her purse and took out a small spiral pad of paper and a pen and scribbled two words: I'm sorry.

Tears blinded her; instinct led her out the bedroom, down the stairs, and to the foyer. She stopped, glanced around her, and then stepped through the door for the final time.

Chapter 20

Lisa hurried to Cynthia's apartment, needing the warmth and support of her best friend. Knocking on her buddy's apartment door, she said aloud, "Come on, Cyn. I need you. Please be home."

Within minutes the chain rattled and the door swung open. "Lisa!" Cynthia exclaimed. Curiosity changed to worry when she examined the pain on her friend's face. She wrapped an arm around Lisa's shoulders and drew her inside the apartment. "What's going on? Are you okay?"

Lisa followed her friend, waiting patiently as Cynthia relocked the door. Cynthia led her to the living room and pushed her onto the sofa, grabbed the remote, and switched off the television. She sank into the spot next to Lisa, taking her hand between both of hers. Examining her face, she asked, "What's happened? Are your folks all right?"

"They're fine."

"Then what happened?" Cynthia asked. "What's wrong?"

"I broke it off with Matthew."

Cynthia shut her eyes, let out a heavy sigh, and shook her head. "Oh, Lisa. Why?"

"I can't marry him. I can't." She swallowed hard, twisting her finger around the gold chain at her neck. "I told you that one day he'll regret being with me. That he'll want something more and I can't give it to him."

A sorrowful expression marred Cynthia's features. "It's time for you to get over that. Grow up."

"I don't understand. What do you mean?" A confused gaze sparkled from Lisa's brown eyes.

"I'm your friend. And friends tell each other the truth regardless of how much it hurts. I love you. But I can't let you continue this way. You have the love of a man that puts you above everything. And all I've heard from you is whining. I can't have babies. He'll regret marrying me," Cynthia mimicked. "You're not the only woman in the world with this problem. It's time you accept it and get on with life."

"I know I'm not. But—but this is about Matthew. Not me."

Cynthia snorted. "No, my friend. It's not. You're punishing yourself and Matthew over something that neither of you is responsible for."

No, you're wrong," Lisa denied. "Think about it. I mean, I think he feels sorry for me but doesn't know how to get out of things."

"Lisa, Matthew runs a multimillion-dollar company. Do you really believe he doesn't know how to solve his problems? You don't think he knows how to get out of things gracefully? He asked you to marry him. No one put a gun to his head and forced him to say anything to you. If Matthew wanted out of the relationship, he's had plenty of time to do so. But he didn't. You were more important to him."

Cynthia's explanation made so much sense. But the fear of rejection kept Lisa from accepting her friend's reasons. "I don't want to marry him, then later find out that he regrets that decision."

"You can't make predictions on what Matthew might do in the future," Cynthia stated. "Live your life for now."

"Oh, Cyn," she cried. "I don't know."

"Well, I do. This is all about you. How *you* feel. How *you* can't have babies. How *you* want to save Matthew from a life without children. He needs to find someone who can provide him with an heir. It's all about you and your fears."

"You don't understand." Lisa jumped to her feet, pacing the room. "When everything is said and done, this is best for Matthew."

Folding her arms across her chest, Cynthia asked, "Best for Matthew? Lisa, you're not his keeper. You're marrying him, not running his life."

"I'm not his keeper. I love him and I want the best for him," Lisa explained.

Sighing, Cynthia asked, "What makes you the expert? You've had one long-term relationship before Matthew. Now you think you have all the answers?"

"I was naive and confused when I got involved with Stephen Brock. He was a mistake. I'm trying to save us both a lot of pain. I never loved Brock the way I love Matthew."

"Then why are you screwing up the greatest thing that ever happened to you? Stop being afraid. Take the leap of faith and love this man with everything in you."

"I can't," Lisa whined.

Cynthia watched her pace the floor and shook her head sorrowfully. "I've never believed you were a coward. But you are."

"I'm not," Lisa snapped. "You don't know what you're talking about."

"Oh, I think I do."

Cynthia came to a decision. Slowly rising from the couch, she stepped into Lisa's path. "I've let you whine and moan long enough. You need to stop. Grow up. Life is hard for all of us. Not just you."

Lisa stood in front of Cynthia, fighting back tears. No one understood what she was going through.

"You've got a man who loves you. Let me repeat that, *loves you* no matter what. No exception, no rules other than the fact that he loves you and wants to spend his life with you. Why are you determined to throw it all away?"

"You don't know what I'm going through. You're just mad at David so you're lashing out at me," Lisa rationalized.

Pain etched Cynthia's features and Lisa was immediately sorry for her harsh words.

"You're right, I'm upset at the way David treated me; he's hurt and humiliated me. Plus, I don't know where we're headed." She shrugged, feeling despair so deep she didn't believe it would ever go away. "But I still want *you* to be happy. What I really want is for all of us to be happy."

Cynthia's confession acted like a slap to the face, jerking Lisa from her mode of self-pity. She shook her head as if she were clearing it. For the first time in weeks, she examined Cynthia, really looked at her. The pain and loneliness were recognizable.

"Oh, Cyn." Lisa hugged her friend. "I'm so sorry. I have been a fool. I should be comforting you."

"It's all right. I know you've been going through a lot."

Her faint smile held a trace of sadness and self-doubt. "We both have, but that's not enough of an excuse." Lisa shook her head and chuckled sadly.

"What?" Cynthia asked.

"We're quite a pair, aren't we?" Lisa asked.

"Yes, we are," Cynthia agreed.

Lisa reached out and took Cynthia's hand. "What are you going to do?"

"I'm so scared. I've got a baby that will be affected by whatever decision David and I make." Tears touched Cynthia's eyes, but she refused to allow them to fall. Turning away, she stared out the window, until she could control the urge to cry.

Pulling her friend into her arms, Lisa held her, wanting Cynthia to draw strength from her. "Don't give up on David yet. He's a good guy. He's just acting real dumb right now."

Giggling, Cynthia drew back. "I agree."

"David's no fool. He'll get it together and you'll work things out. I'm sure of that."

"Are you?" Cynthia sighed, then admitted in a calm, rational voice, "I'm not so sure. I'm beginning to wonder if we should be together."

"Cynthia Williams, you love him and he loves you."

"I know that. But loving each other doesn't always mean we'll end up together."

"Oh, Cyn, don't think like that," Lisa warned. "There's a lot going on in your life and I want you to know that if you need me, I'm here."

"Thank you. But I'll survive. I always have and I always will. I want to get back to you for a minute. Don't throw away everything." She raised her hand in a halting gesture. "Pump the brake, stop, and think about your future and what you want out of life."

"How about you do the same?" Lisa challenged. "I know David's on the top of your bad list and I don't blame you. When you finally talk to him, hear him out before you make your final decision. Promise me," Lisa demanded. "Come on, promise me."

Placing a hand over her heart, Cynthia said, "I promise."

The continual ringing of the doorbell exploded in Matthew's head and roused him from his drunken slumber. Cursing, he rose from the bed and stumbled over his shoes. "What the hell!" he swore, gripping the bedpost to steady himself.

He stood, wavering as he tried to pull a coherent thought from the brain cells that he hadn't killed off with cognac. Once again, the doorbell exploded inside his head, making his head beg for a bottle of aspirin or another drink.

Gingerly making his way into the hallway, Matthew used the walls for support as he headed for the staircase. The stairs seemed to shift under his feet as he tried to get down the steps without killing himself.

"Whoa!" he muttered, gripping the banister as he descended the remaining stairs. Matthew held his forehead, wishing the idiot on the other side of the door would blow into a zillion pieces the next time he touched the doorbell.

Clinging to the wall, he stumbled through the foyer and flung the door open after disarming the alarm. He gazed at the woman standing proudly on his porch, the point of her shoe tapping the concrete impatiently. Cynthia Williams. What was she doing here?

Great! he thought, opening the door wider so that she could come in. Her floral fragrance made him gag as she passed him. Hadn't he suffered enough indignities for one day? But it looked as if he must endure more. First, Lisa had dumped him and now her friend stood at his door while he tried to recover from his alcoholic haze of self-pity. Standing taller, he tried to maintain a bit of dignity in front of his employee.

"Cynthia," Matthew muttered, turning away from the door and staggering to the living room.

"Well, I see you're not in the best of moods," she stated.

Matthew waved a hand in her direction and continued down the hallway. "Cynthia, you've caught me at a really bad time. Unless this is an urgent matter, let's table it until tomorrow at work, okay?"

He entered the room and flopped down on the sofa.

Before she left home, she had it all worked out in her head. Seeing him this way made her nervous and hesitant about interfering in their affairs. Now she questioned her decision to come here.

Following him, Cynthia stood over the sofa, waiting for him to talk to her. She gave him a scalding examination before saying, "You look like day-old garbage and I smell liquor. This isn't like you."

"No, it's not," he mumbled, feeling the cutting edge of regret. What was he going to do? How was he going to get Lisa back? Leaving her engagement ring on the bedside table seemed so final. He didn't know how to convince her that they could work things out.

The sharp morning sun skewed him with a beam of blinding light. Quickly, he shut his eyes and tossed an arm over his face. Cynthia walked around the coffee table and took the chair across the room. She crossed her legs at the ankles, studying him. "I'm here to help. Tell me what I can do."

Matthew peeked at her from under his arm. "There's nothing you can do. I appreciate the fact that you want to help." He burrowed his face farther into the sofa. "Thanks for dropping by. Go home."

"There's always hope, Matthew. It's only over if you want it to be." She rose, folding her arms across her chest.

"The love of my life decided she couldn't marry me. I'm too tired. Let me get some rest and maybe later I can talk about Lisa and me. Now isn't the time." He rose and started for the doorway.

Nodding, she left him and crossed the foyer. She closed the front door behind her and went to her car. She hadn't gained a thing by going there. For several minutes she sat, tapping out a tune on the steering wheel. Matthew and Lisa were champions of stubbornness.

What those two needed was a diversion that would bring them together and allow them to air their differences. She should lock them in the conference room and leave them there until they agree to work out their problems. A smile formed on Cynthia's lips as the first seeds of a plan formed in her head.

Chapter 21

Frustrated, David slammed the telephone back into its cradle. "That's the last time I call her," he promised himself, heading to the refrigerator. He opened a bottle of scotch and poured the liquor over ice cubes. Grabbing a remote from the desk, he turned on the television.

Each night for the past week he'd returned to the hotel and called Cynthia, using every persuasive tool at his command to cajole his way back into her good graces. Nothing had worked.

Each night their stilted conversation ended the same way; they exchanged pleasantries about the weather and the state of the economy but engaged in no meaningful dialogue. She'd chatted with him but shied away from any decision making that related to their relationship or a new date for their wedding. With the baby on the way, he expected her to be eager to reschedule. Instead, she'd skillfully dodged every attempt he made to pin her down to a specific date.

What more did Cynthia want? Apologizing hadn't worked. If they were going to have any quality of life, his career required an occasional sacrifice. This case would cement their future and they could live any place, anywhere, and any way they chose.

Flopping down on the bed with the glass of scotch in his hand, David reached for his portfolio. There were fifteen additional depositions to complete before he returned to Chicago.

"At the top of the hour we'll discuss the ongoing legal woes of Dytech Technologies," announced the CNN news anchor. David turned to the TV, eager to hear what the newscaster had to report. A commercial detailing information about a GMAC truck-leasing program filled the television screen as he sipped his drink. David's eyes strayed to the list of witnesses the opposing counsel had deposed. He pondered each person's importance while running through a mental list of questions his adversaries might ask.

Something's not right, he thought, scanning a list of Dytech employees. There was a discrepancy, but he wasn't sure what. Where was that list Autumn had supplied? He needed to compare the two because he remembered more employees from his assistant's list.

David leaped off the bed and moved across the room to his briefcase. He popped the lock, rummaged inside, and produced a single sheet of paper. The document from human resources listed all the employees who handled the company's pension fund. His forehead scrunched into a frown as he reviewed the list.

Autumn's original list and the most recent one from Dytech were slightly different. William Rimmer, Kevin Jones, and Serena Minor were missing from Dytech's list. What happened to them? David scratched his head, speculating on one or two unsavory explanations for the employees' disappearances.

He searched every legal document from Dytech, but there wasn't an explanation for the missing employees. Reaching for the telephone, he dialed Autumn's number.

"Good afternoon, you've reached the office of David Daniels. May I help you?" Autumn answered.

"Hey. It's me. I've got a job for you."

"Great. It's incredibly boring around here without you."

"I've got three people from Dytech that I need you to locate. Get me phone numbers and addresses. I want Albert to find them and do interviews."

"Sorry. Albert went on sick leave. We'll have to get another investigator to do this."

"Mmmm." David took a long swallow of scotch. He trusted Albert's judgment more than anyone's. He needed another person that could deliver high-quality work. Whom could he trust?

"Get me Simon Broderick's cell phone number. He works for the firm. His reputation is clean and good."

"Hold on. Let me look in the company directory."

David reached for a pen and paper from the desk and copied the number as Autumn recited it. He thanked Autumn, but before he could hang up, she asked, "How's Miss Williams?"

"Fine. Why do you ask?"

"Just wondering how things are between you since you flew to Philadelphia."

"Things are a little tense."

Autumn's chuckle filtered through the phone lines. "I imagine so. Hope everything works itself out. I'll talk to you once I have more info."

"Thanks," he muttered into the dead phone line before hanging up.

Wasting little time, he dialed Simon Broderick's number. He picked up on the fifth ring. "Simon, this is David Daniels."

"Oh, Mr. Daniels. How are you?"

"Fine."

"Is this about your fiancée?" Simon asked. "I've got some info, but I'm still piecing things together."

"I need to hear about that, but I also want you to do another job for me. Sorry, not me, the company. My investigator went on sick leave and I need a professional to do some work on the Dytech case."

"Wow. High-profile stuff. What do you want me to do?"

"There are three employees that disappeared from Dytech's employee rosters. They're not showing up on anything I have. Find them. Learn why they're not on the witness list and get their stories."

"I can do that. How soon?"

"Yesterday."

"Does that mean you want me to stop working on the other project?"

"No. Remember, that was after hours, so continue after hours."

"Cool."

"Speaking of that case, what have you learned?"

"I've got the mother's Social Security number. I'm going to run it through a few databases to see what pops up. Once I've determined that it's her, I'll check the location and let you know what I find."

"Good, good." David didn't want some strange woman using her maternal connection to Cynthia to upset their life. Honestly, he'd already upset their life enough with his job.

"Thanks, Simon. Call me once you learn something on either case."

He hung up and made his way back to the bed. Those missing employees worried him. Things didn't feel right. Something was definitely off.

Sitting on the edge of the bed, he considered the happenings in his life. No wedding. Cynthia was upset with him and he'd bet his next month's salary that his parents were going to disown him when he got home. He stretched out on the bed, fighting the feeling that his life was spiraling out of control. When he accepted this case, he had envisioned a corner office on the top floor, a partnership, and prestige.

Lately, he felt disconnected from everything he held dear, Cynthia, his family—even the values that were such an intricate part of him were fading as the job took on more and more importance. Ruffino, Hartman and Black had always been good to him. Now he felt as if he were losing himself in its grip.

On top of that, he missed Cynthia.

"Hi, Cyn," Jacob's excited voice zipped through

the telephone line. Something was up, she could tell from the way he said her name. He always called her Cynthia, yet today he'd abbreviated her name.

"Hey," she responded, fighting the urge to question him. She perched on the edge of her leather chair, sipping her glass of milk, and waited. He would tell her in his own good time. She'd learned one thing about him over the last few weeks of their working together. Jacob got things done when he was ready and not before.

"I found your mother. I got an address and telephone number for her."

Cynthia gasped, then stood straight up. Her heart rate increased to an alarming level.

"Are you still there?" Jacob asked.

"Yeah," she pushed out from stiff, cold lips. "Yes, I'm here. I didn't expect you to get the information so quickly."

"Hey. That's what I do." He chuckled. "I know it's a shock. But I got a break once we got her Social Security number. That led me to her."

"Mmm," she muttered, still too rattled to add much to this one-sided discussion. "How do you know it's her?"

"I called."

"Called! Did you talk to her? Tell her about me?" Cynthia held her breath.

"Hey," Jacob returned with pride, "I'm a pro. I'm discreet and I protect my clients. It's my job to determine the accuracy of my information."

"Sorry. Didn't mean to offend you."

"It's okay. For your information, I told her I was

from the voting bureau and needed to confirm her residential address before the next election."

She let out a ragged breath.

"So, here's the deal. I've got her address and telephone number. You can possibly call her, make with the small talk, tell her who you are, then move to setting up a meeting with her."

"Jacob, is she here?" Cynthia held her breath. "I mean does she live in Chicago?"

"Nope. Your mother is originally from Detroit. And that's where she lives now."

His words rolled around and around in her head. "Then how did she leave me in Chicago?"

"I'm still working on that," he answered.

"No, don't worry about it. That's something we can discuss." Cynthia licked her lips and asked, "What else did you find out?"

"She's a nurse who works in the Detroit metro area."

Cynthia smiled. It felt good to think of her as a compassionate person that cared for others. She liked that idea.

Jacob's voice zipped through the telephone line. "So what do you want to do?"

That's was a good question. Her thoughts immediately turned to David as sadness filled her. This was an event she should be sharing and celebrating with him. They should be booking a flight to Detroit together. When she met her family, David should be at her side. She was still upset by his actions, but she couldn't deny that she missed him.

"I checked the airlines and the hotels. It's less than an hour's flight. By the time we get in the air, we're almost ready to land. Northwest's flights leave here all day long. Do you want me to book one for us?" Jacob asked.

She'd forgotten that he was on the line and asked in a confused tone, "What?"

"When do you want to leave? I can set everything up and we can get out of town in the next day or so."

If David wouldn't be with her, she would do this alone. Meeting her mother would be a delicate matter at best; add the baby and her lack of a groom, and Cynthia knew she didn't need anything more to upset her new family.

"Jacob, thank you for everything but I think this part I want to do by myself."

"But—"

"Wait," she began. "Please listen. I need to meet my mother on my own. This is going to be difficult enough with my trying to explain who I am and what's going on in my life without adding more stuff."

"I'm stuff?"

She heard the pain in his voice. "No, I'm sorry. Words are coming out of my mouth, but they're not making any sense. I'm not thinking. There's so much to consider. I'm a bit afraid and I want to do this without an audience. I appreciate everything you've done for me, but I think the best chance for my mother and me to get to know one another, to bond, is for us to be alone."

"All right," Jacob responded. "I'm here if you need me."

"Thank you."

After hanging up, Cynthia wandered through

her apartment and finally entered her bedroom. She moved around the room, smoothing the bedspread, fluffing the pillows as she considered her next move.

Everything had come together so quickly and she felt so many emotions. Elation, fear, happiness. Finally, she would have the answers to all the questions that had haunted her all of her life. Why had her mother abandoned her? Where was her father throughout her mother's turmoil? Did she have grandparents? Where were they throughout this? Did they know about her existence? Where were her grandparents? In Chicago or Detroit?

What about siblings? Did she have any? Her years among the Daniels clan made her crave a connection. A brother or sister would be nice. Siblings like the Danielses who loved and supported one another. Someone she could confide in and become friends with, develop a relationship like the one she had with Lisa.

What about her father? Who was he? Hopefully, her mother would be able to answer that question.

Then there were questions that had nothing to do with her parentage. She wanted to know more about her mother, her work, and her life. Cynthia wanted to know everything.

Who do I resemble? My mother? Or my father?

Cynthia ran a hand through her hair. *Does my mother have hair the same color as mine?* she wondered. This was a great adventure filled with awe and she planned to get all the information she'd ever wanted during her trip to Detroit.

Chapter 22

"Hey, girl," Cynthia called, opening the door wider. "Come on in."

Lisa stepped over the threshold and wrapped a warm arm around Cynthia's shoulder, drawing her close. For a minute they held each other, enjoying the silent renewal of their relationship.

Releasing her, Cynthia shut the door, strolled through the house, and headed to the kitchen.

"Whoo, baby! What are you cooking?" Lisa halted in the hallway that led to the kitchen, sniffing the air appreciatively. "Fish. Fried fish. All right! And I smell tomatoes, oregano, and garlic." The tip of her tongue settled in the corner of her mouth. "Spaghetti, right?"

Cynthia nodded.

"You've never been a cook. What brought this on?"

"A baby that seems to make me stay hungry."

"Hey! Don't put that hunger thing on my niece or nephew. You're just plain greedy and trying to pretend it's the baby."

Lisa sounded so natural and carefree. Cynthia

studied her friend's soft, relaxed features. "You're all right with the baby, aren't you?"

"Yeah. Yes, I am. Don't get me wrong. I'd be lying if I denied that I get a twinge of envy periodically. But I can't hide from my life forever. It's time for me to move on. And I want that to be with Matthew."

"Are you ready to live that life with Matthew? I mean really live it?"

"You know I am, thanks to you."

With a smile on her face, Cynthia hugged Lisa. "Good. I didn't do anything."

Lisa dropped her purse on the kitchen table and pulled out a chair. Sinking into it, she made herself comfortable. "Right, Miss Innocent. All you did was fake a meeting that got Matthew and me talking. You didn't do a thing."

Cynthia examined Lisa while humming to Barry White's "Baby, We Better Try to Get It Together." Her buddy looked really good, happy and relaxed. Happiness radiated from her like a beacon.

She moved to the stove with a fork in her hand and tested the fish frying in the black cast-iron skillet, then returned to the table. A grin spread across her face. "Obviously, it worked."

"Yes, it did!" Lisa muttered, giggling as if they were high school students discussing the intricate details of their first kisses. "Matthew and I are back together. We worked things out."

"Sweet." She hugged Lisa close. "I always told you that Matthew was the one for you and too fine to be left alone. Men like him are at a premium and believe me, there are plenty of hungry sistahs out there waiting for you to make a mistake. You'd better snatch him up while the snatching is good."

Cynthia rose from the table and went to the refrigerator. Removing a Coke and a pitcher of orange juice, she filled a glass with her beverage, returned to the table, and slid the can of Coke across the table to Lisa.

"Thanks," Lisa muttered, popping the tab. "It took me a while but I finally figured out what you guys have been trying to make me understand. You and Matthew tried to help me come to terms with my limitation. But I wasn't ready to listen. I can be quite the stubborn chick when the notion hits me," she admitted in a self-mocking tone. "And I almost lost Matthew because of that."

"Matthew's true blue. You couldn't lose him even if you tried." Her eyebrows rose significantly. "Well, you did try. He stuck right there with you, didn't he?"

Nodding, Lisa turned away and admitted in a small, uncomfortable voice, "I pushed him away and hurt him in ways that I can't explain. I did a lot of damage that I'm going to have to repair."

"If you do it with a lot of love, he'll forgive you. So take off that sorrowful expression and get happy. The man loves you dearly and you love him more."

"Yes, I do." Lisa nodded eagerly.

"Good. How are you feeling about not having kids?" Cynthia asked in a quiet, concerned tone.

"It's an ache that never truly goes away. I know that now." She drew a deep breath and added, "A child can't take the place of the love of a man.

Matthew is a part of me and I don't want to live without him or his love."

Cynthia reached across the table and squeezed Lisa's hand. "You don't have to."

"Thank you for trying to make me see how I was screwing up my life. I don't know if I've told you this lately, but I appreciate everything you tried to do for me during that time. Not just that time, but for always being my friend."

"You're my best friend. And I love you dearly. I want you to be happy."

"Thanks." Lisa glanced around the room. "Speaking of happy, what about you? You have a glow about you that I suspect has nothing to do with the baby."

"I've got some good news recently."

Lisa shifted around in her chair. "What kind of news? Tell me about it."

"I've found my mother."

Lisa's eyes grew large and round. "Ohmigod! Ohmigod!" She shook her head and said again, "Ohmigod! When? How?"

"When was a few days ago. How . . ." Cyn gave Lisa a big cheesy smile. "Matthew's friend Jacob, I recruited him to help me locate my mother."

"Why did you do this? Why now?"

"I never told you. This is the deep, dark secret I've refused to share until now. But I've always wanted to know who my mother was. She left me and I want to know why."

"I can see that. How come you didn't search for her years ago? Like right after we graduated from high school? Why didn't you tell me? Maybe I could have helped."

"For a long time I was afraid to take this big a step. I didn't really know how to go about finding her."

"But why now?"

"Because I'm going to have a baby and along with wanting to know who my mother is, I need to know her medical history."

"That makes sense," Lisa conceded. "Does my brother know about this?"

Cynthia glanced away. "Some of it."

"What's going on with my wayward brother and you? Have you guys settled your issues? I mean, you are going to have a baby in a few months. It would be nice for my nephew's parents to be married."

"I haven't heard from him in a couple of days. I guess he's okay."

"You don't know?"

Cynthia shrugged. "I don't want to talk about David. Let's talk about something a bit more interesting."

Lisa raised her hands palms-up in an act of surrender. "I won't pursue it."

"Thank you," Cynthia muttered.

"Are you afraid?"

"A little. More excited than anything. You've always had parents that have been part of your life. You take their presence for granted. I've always envied you for that. I'm not jealous. I just wanted my own parents that loved me for who I am just like you have."

"Cyn, they're your family too. You're my sister just as much as Vee. I love you both."

"I know you do. And everyone treats me like family. But it's your family. Not mine. It was never mine. You let me in, but I was never truly part of things."

"You're wrong. Ma and Dad love you like one of us. We all do."

Cynthia offered a sad smile that revealed how little she believed Lisa's words. "Maybe they do. Latonya Williams will love me and that's what I want. Please understand this has nothing to do with your parents or the feelings I have for them and you. I want my own family. People like me who look like me."

"I'm going to say something that I don't want you to take the wrong way. I just want you to think about it and consider it." Lisa drew in a deep breath before continuing, "Have you thought about the fact that your mother has not contacted you since she dropped you off over twenty years ago? She's never tried to find you. Doesn't that indicate anything?"

Cynthia rose from the table and stopped in front of her stove. She removed the crisp fillets of fish from the skillet, placing them on a platter covered with a white paper towel. "I thought about it," she admitted quietly. "There could be a bunch of reasons why she's never found me. I mean, maybe she couldn't find me. The foster care agency may not have given her any information to locate me. She could have tried and maybe it didn't work out. There could be a half dozen reasons why she hasn't found me."

"Is Jacob sure this is your mother? I mean"—Lisa swallowed hard—"does he have proof?"

"Yes. He did research and then he followed everything up on the Internet, plus a phone call. That's how he found her."

"What are you going to do?"

"I'm going to Detroit to meet her. I plan to talk with her."

"Oh, Cyn." Lisa's look of dismay was almost comical. "Are you sure this is the right thing to do?"

"Yes."

"I don't want to discourage you, but I do want you to be careful. This lady may not want you in her life. She could have a new family that she doesn't want to know about her past and you. Promise me that you'll take things slow."

"You're wrong. I'll be fine. We're going to be a family. Friends."

"Maybe you should talk with my folks. Tell them what you're planning and get their opinion on how you should proceed. They've always given you sound advice in the past and you've always respected their opinion. It couldn't hurt."

"Miss Helen and Mr. Nick have always been supportive of me and my choices in life and I value that. But this is my stuff. It's about my life, who I am and where I came from. I don't want to get your parents involved with that."

"But they're your family, too, and they care."

"Not really. They've always treated me like a member of your tight clan. But I know different. I've always been an outsider. It's nobody's fault. It's the way things are."

"I never realized that you felt that way. I'm sorry. I always thought of you as my sister."

"Thank you. Lisa, you are my sister."

"If this search is that important to you, then I want you to get the answers you need. But if you're wrong, you could ruin some woman's life. Be very careful and make sure you've got the correct woman."

"I trust Jacob. If he's sure, then I believe him."

"Jacob is very thorough." Lisa twisted her engagement ring around her finger. "I'll tell you what. I'll come with you. I've never been to Detroit and this would be the best time for me. Give me a date and we'll fly out together."

"You can't. You and Matthew just got back together and I'm not going to disrupt that. You guys need time together. Besides, this is my thing. I've got to do this alone."

"I—I—I," Lisa stammered.

Cynthia shook her head, smiling to take the sting out of her words. "Don't look so stricken. I know what I'm doing. Honestly. Now, while I'm gone, you start planning that wedding and I'll take care of my business. Remember, I'll be having a baby and you better not wait until I'm almost ready to deliver to get married."

"Yeah, right." Lisa examined Cynthia with the practiced eye of a connoisseur. "Although I have to admit you're the skinniest pregnant lady I've seen. Cyn, is everything all right? I mean, it doesn't look as if you've gained a pound."

"I know. I'm going to schedule another appointment with Dr. Noah before I leave town. I'll ask him about things."

Nodding, Lisa said, "Good."

Humming to Anita Baker's "Giving You the Best That I've Got," Cynthia answered her phone. "Hello?"

"Ms. Williams?"

"Yes."

"This is April from Dr. Noah's office calling. How are you?"

"I'm good." Anxiously, Cynthia sank into the chair next to the phone. Heat surged up her neck and she laid a protective hand over her belly. Swallowing hard, she forced down a lump the size of Kansas and waited. "What can I do for you?"

"Your test results are back, including the ultrasound, and Dr. Noah would like to have you come into the office to see him."

"When?" Cynthia asked with fear in her heart.

"Would Tuesday morning at nine work for you?" April asked.

"Yes."

"Take care, Ms. Williams. We'll see you Tuesday."

Smothering a sob, Cynthia placed the telephone on the end table and brushed away tears. The last week had been brutal. She had endured a canceled wedding and the constant and sometimes insincere condolences from some of her friends and colleagues. The most difficult to endure were David's calls.

He called each evening trying to explain why he

hadn't made it to the wedding. Her feelings were too raw to discuss the situation. Instead, they made small talk until he got tired and hung up. A second wave of tears painted her cheeks and Cynthia hurried to her bedroom for tissues.

Her appointment with Dr. Noah frightened her beyond anything she could describe. She suspected he planned to tell her that she wasn't pregnant or there was something wrong with the baby. Shutting her eyes, she wondered how much more she'd have to endure before this nightmare ended.

Chapter 23

Cynthia scooped her toiletries from her bathroom sink into her cosmetics bag. With a practiced gaze she scanned the room, searching for additional items that she might need on her trip. She returned to her bedroom and headed for her closet, sliding garment after garment across the clothes rod, examining each item for appropriateness. She didn't need anything elaborate, just one or two comfortable pieces for her days in Detroit.

Once she finished her appointment with Dr. Noah, she'd take a train to the city. *If my mother has family in Detroit, maybe I'll get to meet them. And I'll need something a bit more dressy for that event,* she thought, searching through her closet.

"This will do," Cynthia muttered, removing a form-fitting pearl silk dress. She placed it on the bed, then got on all fours to search for a pair of matching low-heel pumps. Retrieving the shoes, Cynthia returned to the closet for a pair of slacks and a top.

How would her mother look? She tried to conjure an image of her new family. Instead, a mental picture of the Danielses and Miss Helen and Mr.

Nick came to mind. She shook her head, trying to dislodge their images, but failed to do so. They'd been such a major part of her life for so long, they would always be present in her thoughts.

She smiled, feeling anticipation course through her. This time tomorrow evening she would be meeting her mother for the first time. All she needed to do was pick up her ticket at Union Station.

Cynthia's eyes settled on the photograph of David sitting on the nightstand next to her bed and her good cheer evaporated. What had happened to them? Six months ago, nothing could have shaken the foundation of their relationship. Yet, now they were very close to separating forever.

She picked up the frame and traced his strong, stubborn chin with her finger. What was she going to do about that man? She loved him with all her heart, but she still felt unconvinced that they were meant to be together forever. Pregnancy didn't fit into this equation. It looked as if they might be headed in different directions with very separate goals. She didn't have a clue as to how to bring them back together. Or if they should be together? David didn't understand her needs. He'd always known the warmth of belonging and having a family, a supportive family that cheered his every accomplishment. He'd never been alone with no one to turn to.

Returning the frame to the nightstand, she deliberately turned off any thoughts regarding David and his clan. Cynthia returned to her packing. This would be the single most important trip of her life and she planned to make it a success.

She removed undergarments from her dresser and started back to the bed when the doorbell rang. Who could that be? She wasn't expecting anyone. Lisa was the only person who knew she was heading out tomorrow morning.

Dropping her things on the bed, she made her way down the hallway to the front door. She stood on tippytoes, looking through the peephole. Jacob, she thought as a jolt of surprise shot through her. She wrinkled her forehead. What did he want?

Cynthia unlocked the door and flung it open. "Hi."

"Hey," he returned. "May I come in?"

Stepping back, she said, "Sure."

He looked so fierce. Maybe he had uncovered additional info for her. Once he stepped into her apartment, she locked the door and said, "What's up?" Fear replaced the previous surge of happiness and expectation. "Is something wrong?"

"No. Relax." He reached out and stroked her arm. "I wanted to talk with you before you leave town."

His touch felt wrong and she took a step away, moving to the living room. She blew out a hot puff of air. "You scared me for a minute. I thought you might be here to tell me that you made a mistake. Let's go in the living room."

He followed her down the hallway.

Waving a hand at the sofa, she offered, "Have a seat."

"Thanks."

Perching on the edge of her chair, she asked, "So what's going on? Why are you here?"

"I'm not sure how to begin, but I'm going to lay things out."

"Okay," she answered slowly, watching Jacob very closely. His face was a mask of conflicting emotions.

He took her hand and held on to it, squeezing her fingers. "I don't want you to go to Detroit alone. This is too important an event. You should have someone with you."

She smiled, pulling her hand free. "Jacob, don't worry about me. I'm a big girl. I've been on my own for a long time. Relax, I'll be fine."

"This is huge. You're going to see your mother for the first time. Are you sure you can handle all the emotional stuff alone?"

"Everything is organized. I've got my train ticket and my hotel reservation. I'm going to stay at the Hyatt in Dearborn. That's close to the train station. There's nothing to worry about. I'll be fine."

"Are you? Are you ready?" Jacob ran a hand through his hair.

"What do you mean?"

"Anything can happen. Are you sure you can handle things?"

"Yes," Cynthia answered. *Where was all of this leading?* she wondered.

"Let me come with you."

"No."

"I understand you and David have been together for years, but I also know that things aren't going well."

She held up a hand, trying to stop him. "Wait—"

"No, let me finish. Just keep an open mind. We've had fun together, right?"

Cynthia nodded.

"Plus, we enjoy some of the same things."

She didn't like where this was going. But she allowed him to finish.

"If you give us, I mean you and me, a chance, I think we can be good together. Really good."

Cynthia shut her eyes, searching for the least painful way to let Jacob down. She liked him, yes. But she didn't care for him in the way he wanted. She hated hurting him. Without his help, it would have been almost impossible to find her parents.

"Jay, please."

"Wait. I like you. That's the whole of it. And I believe, if you let yourself, maybe you'll admit that you have feelings beyond friends for me."

"I like you. But not romantically. You're my friend and I don't want to lose you over this."

"I want more."

She shook her head. "I'm sorry. I can't give you that. If I've led you on, that wasn't my intention. You see, David is still in my heart. And whether we get back together or not, he's still the man I love."

"Even though he's not here? Went off to do his own thing, and you still believe he loves you?"

"I can't control David's feelings and they're not an issue here. I'm telling you about my feelings. Whether he loves me or not, I still love him and we will always be connected because of this baby. I can't change that."

A self-mocking smile crossed Jacob's face. "Matthew tried to tell me. Okay, maybe I have to accept that. But don't forget, I'm your friend and I'll always be around if you need me."

"Thank you."

"Well, you're still my priority and meeting your mother for the first time is huge. Are you sure you don't want someone along for moral support? What about Lisa? Could she go with you?"

"No. I don't know how to explain things to you. But I think I'm going about this the right way. Meeting her will be a difficult situation, but I don't want to scare my mother. I'd like it to be intimate, just the two of us. There's so much I want to know and I don't think she'll open up with other people around."

Nodding, Jacob stood. "I see your point. At least think about having Lisa along. She can stay at the hotel while you visit your mother."

She stood and hugged him close. "Thank you. I never would have found her without your help."

Jacob rubbed her arm and smiled sadly. "My pleasure."

Two pregnancy tests, three tubes of blood, and an ultrasound later, Cynthia waited for Dr. Noah, wrapped in a blue paper hospital gown. As she rubbed a comforting hand across her belly, her thoughts took an unsettling flight of fancy, envisioning all manner of illnesses and problems for herself or the baby. A nervous flutter of queasiness settled in the pit of her stomach. What was wrong?

An avalanche of emotions bombarded her as she considered the consequences of what all these tests meant. Was the baby okay? Or had the test results revealed an unknown medical problem about her?

Dr. Noah stepped into the room after a sharp rap on the door. "Hello. How are you?" He sank onto a stool and wheeled it to where Cynthia sat on the examining table, studying her with a keen, analytical eye.

"I'm fine," she answered, twisting the gown's ties between her fingers.

"Good." He sighed heavily, readjusting the black-rimmed glasses on his nose. "We have things we need to discuss."

"What's going on, Dr. Noah?"

"First of all, the pregnancy test results have come back." He covered her hand with his own and said in a voice laced with regret, "I'm sorry, Cynthia. The results were negative. You're not pregnant."

His words froze in her brain and she shuddered inwardly. Cynthia withdrew her hand and turned away.

Her vision blurred and a sharp humming in her head drummed out all thoughts. Loss, sharp and frightening, punched her in the heart. For weeks she had fought with David about the life she wanted for herself and this baby and now all of that had been reduced to a few words. There was no baby and her life was in a shambles.

Her fist wrapped around a handful of the paper garment while she speared Dr. Noah with a questioning glare. "No, you're wrong. I took a pregnancy test. You said everything looked good." Her voice broke miserably and it took her a moment to recover. "Now you're saying a very different thing."

"And from what I could determine from the initial examination, everything was fine. Unfortunately, it became clear fairly early that something wasn't quite right."

"Why didn't you tell me?" she demanded.

"I wanted to have all the facts before I made any diagnosis. How would you feel if I had told you what I suspected and then found out that I was wrong? I erred on the side of caution."

Cynthia sat in unhappy silence, fighting back tears, shutting her eyes against her changing world. "I don't understand. My home pregnancy test came back positive."

"We call that a false positive."

"False positive?"

He surveyed her kindly before saying, "Yes. Your test indicated that you were pregnant, but it was wrong. A blood test is definitive."

"How can that be?" she asked in a dull and troubled voice. "I mean, my periods have been off for months. What caused that?"

"Any number of things can be responsible. Hormones that are out of whack. Years of using oral contraceptives. Don't underestimate the power of stress. Although, in your case, we've pinpointed the cause."

A gamut of illnesses flew through her mind, and cancer topped the list. "And that is?" Cynthia asked, holding her breath.

"You have a cyst on your left ovary."

"Cyst?"

"Remember when your test results came back negative for pregnancy and you had an ultrasound. Well, we found a small cyst the size of a pencil eraser."

"That's not very big. Is that why I hurt sometimes and my periods have been so strange?"

"Yes."

"What's next? Surgery?" she asked in an anxious whisper.

"No. I've had success with medication. All you'll need is a shot to shrink it."

She blew out a hot puff of air. "A shot?"

He nodded.

Her thoughts swiftly moved to another worrisome question. "What happens when I decide to have kids? Will this cyst become a problem?"

"Not at all. This shot will dissolve the cyst and you'll be fine."

"Good. Dr. Noah, is this something connected to my parents? Could this have come from my mother?"

"I see where you're going with this. There's no clear-cut answer for you. Maybe, maybe not."

"You sound like a politician," she said.

"There's not enough data to make an educated guess. It's certainly something you might want to ask your mother should you meet her."

"Fair enough. I think I will. So, when do we do this shot?"

"Now."

"Now?" she squealed, expecting Dr. Noah to suggest she return to the office next week.

Standing, he opened the door and called, "Cherie, I need you in room four, please."

"On my way," came the disembodied female voice.

Dr. Noah moved to the counter and opened a drawer. He removed a syringe, then took a small bottle of liquid medication from the countertop. "No time like the present."

Cynthia maintained her composure until she reached her vehicle. She fell into the driver's seat as tears ran down her cheeks. Alone in her car, she wept aloud, rocking back and forth.

She felt so empty. The life she dreamed of was gone. Brushing away tears, Cynthia drew in a shaky breath and tried to concentrate on her future.

After weeks of contemplating how this imaginary baby might change her life, she found it difficult to wrap her mind around the fact that she wasn't pregnant. Now her life would change a second time.

Pain squeezed her heart as she thought of David. He was never far from her thoughts and this revelation brought him starkly into focus. How would he react? A cynical smiled filled with sadness touched her lips. No need for them to get married. He'd probably run for the mountains, doing the happy dance along the way.

Maybe this situation had worked out for the best. No baby. No wedding. No permanent complications or problems. She and David were now free to move ahead with their lives. He could pursue his career and leave everyone else behind.

Where did that leave her? What about love? If David didn't want her love, it was time to pursue her interests and make a change in her life. She planned to focus her energy on her career and getting to know her parents. Regret swept through her as she thought of Miss Helen, Mr. Nick, and Lisa. For fourteen years, the Daniels clan had served as the stabilizing force in Cynthia's life.

Now it was time for her to move on and start a new life.

Chapter 24

"This better be important," David warned half-heartedly as he snatched up the telephone. There were still a dozen depositions scheduled for the next few days; plus he needed to review the transcripts from today's deps. "Yeah?"

"David?" Lisa's voice came through the telephone lines loud and clear.

He cocked his head and answered, "Hey?"

"How are you?"

His blood pressure shot up over two hundred and he asked in a shaking voice, "Cynthia? The baby? Is everyone all right? Is something wrong with Cynthia?"

"Calm down. Cyn's okay. Mom, Dad, everyone's fine. I'm sorry, I didn't mean to put a scare into you," her soft, silvery voice reassured him, then she laughed. "Actually, I did. But not about *your* family."

Relieved, he sighed with exasperation and sank onto the bed. He ran his hand over his face, taking a deep breath. If there wasn't anything wrong, why was Lisa calling? She was not the type for idle chatter. "What's going on? Spit it out. Why are you calling?"

"We need to talk about Cyn," Lisa stated in a no-nonsense tone.

"I don't have time for this. I've got a lot of work to do. Say what you need to and let me get back to work."

"David, Cynthia found her mother."

Startled, he stopped, the papers from his briefcase spilling onto the floor. "Her mother? How? When?"

"She hired Matthew's friend Jacob Summers and he found her. She is planning a trip to Detroit to meet her."

"Detroit?"

"Yeah. That's where her mother lives. I don't want her to be alone. You need to be with her and she needs you."

He shook his head dubiously. "I can't. There're still depositions to finish."

"What's more important to you? Your career or your family? It's time to make a choice."

Ruffino's veiled threat kept him immobilized. David glanced around his suite and shook his head. There wasn't a snowball's chance in hell that he could leave right now. "I've got a great deal of responsibility here. I can't just pack up and leave."

There was a long pause from the other end of the telephone. A pause filled with accusations and recriminations. A silence designed to embarrass and admonish him, and it accomplished both. David could just feel Lisa swelling up like a Thanksgiving turkey on steroids, gearing up to put him firmly in his place.

"This is one of the most important moments in

Cynthia's life. You should be there to support her. I would think you would want to be with her," she began in a lofty tone.

"You're right," David admitted. "I should be with her. But Cyn hasn't been exactly happy with me lately."

Lisa snorted. "I'm not happy with you either. You need to put that aside and help her."

"Is that why you called? To get on my ass, give me grief, stir up trouble?"

"No. You're a grown man, you can do whatever you want. I want to help a friend that helped me. It's my turn to help her."

"I don't need this crap."

"Maybe not. David, if you want to fix things between you and Cynthia, supporting her will help."

He groaned, finding it difficult to ignore the truth. Lisa was asking seriously important questions. How long did he plan to allow Ruffino, Hartman and Black to dictate his life? "There's more going on, isn't there?"

"Yes."

"What is it?"

"She's leaving tomorrow morning."

"No."

"Yes! What are you going to do about it? Are you going to support her or continue to worry over your career?"

His heart twisted when he remembered the disappointment marring Cyn's features when he'd had to leave her alone at her first ob/gyn appointment. Her voice pleaded for him to understand when she told him that she needed to keep her job.

He'd ignored her concerns and fears when she confessed that she was pregnant. Cyn shouldn't have had any doubts that he would stand with her. There had been too many times when he'd been a pitiful fiancé. Cynthia deserved so much more. She deserved everything he had and what she'd received was the crumbs of his time and affection.

Something clicked in his head and he realized that he kept giving her everything but himself. His own driving need appalled him. How he'd ignored everyone in pursuit of his own goals. "Do you know where she's staying?"

"Hyatt. Don't delay."

"I won't. It's time for me to get my priorities correct. What about you? Everything okay with you and Matthew?"

"You know what?" Lisa asked.

"What?"

"I've finally figured things out. You can't let anything come between you and the person you love. Not a job, or another person, not even children. You've got to be strong enough to give it your best. Open your heart and take what comes with it."

"I take it you've figured out how to be with Matthew."

"Yeah. And it's good. It's the best thing in my life and my heart almost stops when I think about how close I came to throwing it all away. Just like you." Lisa's comparison hung in the air between them like an executioner's noose.

"Did Cynthia tell you where her mother lives? How about an address?"

"Sorry," Lisa answered. "All I know is she's going to Detroit."

"No problem. I'll put my PI on it. If surfer boy found her location, my PI should be close."

"PI? What PI? . . . Oh, never mind. David, Cyn needs you. Be there for her."

"I will."

"Here are my final words of wisdom. Don't screw up, big bro. Give Cynthia everything you've got."

"Thanks, Little Bit," he muttered into the phone and hung up.

David slammed the phone into its cradle. Where in the hell was Simon? It had been more than an hour since he'd paged him. As he paced the floor, Lisa's words came back to haunt him. He had been unfair to Cynthia, expecting her to understand while he pursued his dreams. He had allowed his job to become so important that nothing else mattered, not even the feelings of the woman he loved the most.

He ran a hand over his chin and rotated his shoulders, trying to relieve the tension building between his shoulder blades. He missed his family, the Sunday get-togethers, Mom's home-cooked meals, card games with J.D. and sitting around shooting the breeze. It had been months since he had been available to participate in any family event. He was either working on a case or out of town. Even when he made it to family functions, he showed up late and missed most of the fun.

More than that, he missed Cynthia. Her passion,

the smile on her face, her quick wit that always put him squarely in his place. Most of all, he missed her love and the way she wrapped herself around him. Her special scent, the feel of her silky skin against his. God, he wanted to make love with her right now.

Picking up the phone, he dialed Ruffino. This was one time he planned to support her. This day and every day after Cynthia would come first.

Chapter 25

There was a knock on the door. David got up from the desk, strolled across the suite, and opened the door to Simon Broderick.

Using two fingers, Simon saluted him. "Hi."

David shook hands with the investigator. "Hey, man. When did you get into town? I just paged you and left at least a half dozen messages on your voice mail."

"I got your page. I was concluding my investigation on those people you wanted me to find. Since I was in town, I decided to stop by your hotel and talk to you about my findings."

"Come on in," David offered, turning back into the suite. "Do you want anything? A drink? Food?"

"A soda would be good. What do you have?" He entered the living room and strolled around the room while examining the hotel setup.

David hid a smile from his investigator. Simon always appeared to be on the job. "Coke, Pepsi, Sprite?"

"Coke."

Simon dropped onto the sofa and shifted around until he got comfortable. David opened the portable refrigerator, removed a bottle of soda, and handed the drink to the other man before taking the chair opposite the investigator.

"We've got a lot to talk about." Simon pulled a small spiral notebook from his back pocket.

"Hold on." David rose from the chair and crossed the room. He snatched a legal pad and pen from the desk and returned to the living room. "Okay, what you got for me?"

Swallowing a good portion of his soda, Simon began, "First of all, it wasn't easy finding these people. They were scattered all over the U.S."

David nodded, listening intently.

"William Rimmer and Kevin Jones—"

David cut Simon off "Wait. I want to hear about Cynthia first. Then we can talk about the case. Did you find Latonya Mason?"

"Yeah," he answered, flipping through his notebook. "Ms. Mason lives in Detroit. She's a nurse at the Detroit Medical Center."

"Do you have a home address for her?"

Simon nodded.

"Good. Is she a good citizen? Pay her bills? Is there any other family?"

"Yeah, yeah, and yeah," Simon answered. "Do you need me to write up a full report?"

"No. I need that address. The rest I can get once I'm back in the office. Hold everything until I get back to Chicago."

"Will do." Simon ripped a sheet from his notebook and handed it to David.

He glanced at the address and nodded. "Hold on. What kind of person is she?"

"Ms. Williams is loved by the people she works with, her neighbors all have good things to say about her. I haven't heard anything negative about her."

Nodding, David stood. "Good. That'll make things easier for Cynthia. Let me get your money." He hurried to the desk and returned with a check.

"Thanks." Simon pocketed the check and rose from the sofa. "Is there anything else you want me to do with either case?"

David chuckled. "Cynthia was my first concern. I forget the case, summarize it."

"I found all three employees. After some serious negotiations I got the info you wanted. Jones is in New York, working for a big accounting firm. He refused to give me anything. William Rimmer and Serena Minor gave me everything I wanted. They pointed the finger at Dytech. Serena had copies of memos and e-mails detailing how the president wanted the pension money rerouted to different accounts."

"Write up your notes. I want the info in their file. Make sure Ruffino and Autumn get copies."

"No problem."

"Good." With a hand on Simon's shoulder, David led him back to the door. "Thanks for your help."

David shut the door after Simon, returned to the living room, and retrieved Latonya Williams's address. He needed to talk with Ruffino, then he could finalize his plans.

David flipped through his yellow legal pad while waiting for someone to pick up the telephone. He added a question here and a note there on the paper.

"Ruffino."

"Mario, this is David Daniels here."

His voice turned friendly and approachable. "Dave, how are things in Philadelphia?"

No point in delaying, David decided, plunging ahead. "That's why I'm calling. I need to leave Philadelphia as soon as possible, sir."

"Oh?" A lengthy silence followed that one word. Finally, Mario spoke. "Is there a problem with the Dytech case?"

"Yes, there is, sir. But that's not why I need to leave. Something personal has come up," he stated with quiet determination. "There's no room for negotiations. I need the time off and I need it now. You need to get someone in here to take the rest of the depositions. I have three scheduled for tomorrow."

David smiled. He could almost feel the wheels turning in Ruffino's head. He wanted to know what had caused this shift in priority so that he could use it against him. That wasn't going to happen.

"Daniels, this is short notice. Can you stay another day?"

He expected Ruffino to ask him to wait. "No. I can't."

"Mmmm. You're making a major request in the middle of a very important case. I thought I made myself clear. You are to handle this case from beginning to end. That was our agreement."

Mario's threats weren't going to work this time.

David was willing to quit his job. He hoped it didn't come to that, but if so, he'd find another.

"I did understand you, sir. That's why I'm here even though it was against my better judgment. But I can't stay."

"It doesn't look good for a potential partner to leave a post in the middle of the night. Do you really think the senior staff will see your deserting us in a favorable light?" Mario was certain he had the upper hand, and his voice carried a smug edge.

This was it. The moment of truth. David had to stand up for himself or he'd be lost forever. "Autumn Snyder has all my notes on the case." David squared his shoulders and said matter-of-factly, "She'll be here in the morning. I suggest you fly one of your senior attorneys here to finish the depositions. I'll be making reservations to leave as soon as I hang up with you. Good night, sir."

David disconnected the call and immediately dialed the airline. There was a flight leaving for Detroit in a couple of hours. He had just enough time to pack and get to the airport. If his plans worked out, he'd be in Detroit in time to go to Latonya Williams's house with Cynthia.

Chapter 26

"Next stop, Dearborn, Michigan," the Amtrak train conductor bellowed, striding along the central aisle of the train.

A flicker of apprehension coursed through Cynthia and her heart skipped several beats. "Almost there," she mumbled low in her throat.

From the train's window, she studied the passing scenery. It moved along the track at a steady pace, offering her a glimpse of Dearborn, Michigan. A soft tingle of wonder floated from her.

A white two-story structure came into view while the gigantic neon sign flashed its welcoming greetings to visitors. The train slowed and she noticed police cars in the parking lot. The Dearborn police station, the library, and the courts shared their location.

Almost there. Finally, many of her dreams were within her grasp. She exhaled a long sigh of contentment.

Her thoughts returned to last night and her final conversation with Jacob. He was the person most instrumental in getting her to this point by providing the information she needed. Jacob's determination made it possible for her to be here today. Her heart felt heavy because she didn't share the feelings he obviously had and wanted from her.

She didn't love Jacob. Could never love him. Although she hadn't been happy with the way David left her, she still loved him. Poor Jacob didn't stand a chance against the intensity of her love for David.

In less than twenty-four hours Cynthia hoped to meet her mother. Possibly have dinner with her and learn the details behind why she'd abandoned her in Chicago.

The train slowed, then stopped outside a small one-story brick structure. The conductor stood on the station platform, offering a supportive hand off the train. Frightened, but determined to find out the truth, she stood on the platform, examining her surroundings. Cynthia gathered her luggage and started for the exit.

According to her itinerary, she was booked at the Hyatt Hotel in Dearborn. She folded her garment bag over her arm and tossed her purse on the other. She entered the station and asked the attendant where she could get a cab. The older gentleman behind the Plexiglas pointed to the door. Three bright orange taxis waited.

She stopped at the first one and peeped into the cab. "Can you take me to the Hyatt?" she asked.

"Yes," the turban-wearing Arabic gentleman answered. "But," and he pointed across the street, "you can walk if you're up to it."

The brown circular top of the Hyatt loomed large and imposing over the other structures in the area. Climbing into the back of the cab, she said,

"I'd rather ride." The cabbie turned right, then completed a left turn onto the fast-moving avenue, heading westward. Cynthia got up the nerve to ask, "How far away is Rosedale Park?"

"Not far at all. Less than ten minutes away. It's north of Michigan Avenue in Detroit," answered the cabdriver.

The cab turned into the circular drive of the Hyatt Hotel. It came to a halt at the lobby entranceway. Cynthia got a good look at the imposing stone and glass structure. She settled the fare and gathered her luggage from the backseat. She strolled into the lush lobby with large floral arrangements, registered, and found her room. Dumping her luggage in a chair, she sank onto the edge of the mattress, feeling disorientated and alone. *David's moral support would come in handy right now,* she thought.

Her gaze strayed to the telephone. Just hearing his voice might do the trick, give her that jolt of adrenaline she needed to take the next step. She lifted the receiver but hesitated. She'd barely spoken to the man in the last few days. Yeah, but she still needed him. Although salvaging their relationship may not be an option any longer, she still loved him and always wanted to stay connected to him and his family.

Gently returning the telephone to its cradle, she resisted her first impulse. She'd made it to this point on her own and needed to keep pushing toward her goals.

The urge to hear a familiar reassuring voice overwhelmed her though. With renewed determination she picked up the telephone and dialed home. The phone rang three times before she heard Miss Helen's voice.

"Hi, Miss Helen," Cynthia greeted, unsure how to proceed. "How are you?"

"Mom! I told you to call me Mom."

"Sorry."

"That's okay. Lisa told me what you're doing. You want to talk about things for a minute?"

Relief filled her. Unburdening herself provided a much-needed opportunity for comfort. "If you don't mind?" she answered with a hopeful note to her voice.

Miss Helen gently admonished her, "Cynthia, you know better. I've always got time for you. You're part of the family."

"I know. Thank you."

"So, how are things going? What about you? Are you feeling okay?"

"Scared." Cynthia twisted a finger around the end of her ponytail.

"That's natural."

Cynthia smiled, feeling Miss Helen's presence as if she were sitting next to her.

"After all, you've got a lot riding on the outcome of this," Mom confirmed.

"Maybe I've made a mistake. I shouldn't have come here."

"Why would you say that? You've put so much time and energy into finding your mother."

"I don't know. Fear of rejection. What if she doesn't like me? What do I do if she doesn't want me in her life?"

Miss Helen laughed. "Cyn, there's no way that's going to happen. You're her daughter and you've grown into a beautiful, talented young woman. You've worked hard to get your bachelor's and master's degrees and you have a wonderful career. Why wouldn't your mother like and love you?

"Thank you."

"Babe, no need to thank me. Whatever happens, we're still here for you. We love you and want you to know that we'll support you. If you need anything, including my coming to Detroit to be with you, just call me. I'll take the next flight out."

"You've always been so good to me, Cynthia choked back tears."

"You're part of my family. And I never let my children down. I'll always be available for you. That's a promise. Now, relax, rest, and get ready for your meeting. This is important. I want you to be comfortable."

"I'll call you after I meet her, okay?"

"Do that. I'll be waiting," Miss Helen replied and then hung up.

Cynthia drew in a deep breath of air and let it out, searching for the calm that would reduce a portion of her stress and the tension that tore at her heart. No guts, no glory, she decided, reaching for her purse, and removed the report Jacob ran for her before she left Chicago.

This meeting would demand finesse on her part. According to Jacob's report, Latonya Mason worked the day shift as a registered nurse for the

Detroit Medical Center. A quick check of the clock radio confirmed her suspicion. Her mother should be home by this time. It took four attempts to get her shaky fingers to punch in the correct combination of numbers. With each ring of the telephone, her belly twisted into tighter and tighter knots.

"Hello?" inquired a teenage boy on the opposite end of the phone line.

Did I dial the wrong number? she wondered, checking the telephone display against the number on Jacob's report. The number was correct. "Hi. Is Latonya Mason in?"

"Who's calling?"

"This is Ms. Williams."

"Hold on. Let me get her."

Cynthia released a shaky sigh of relief and pushed her glasses up her nose. Moisture formed on the back of her neck and forehead. Psyching herself up for the next hurdle, she ran the back of her trembling hand across her forehead.

"Hello?"

Completely paralyzed, Cynthia couldn't speak.

"Hello?"

"H-h-h-hi," she stammered. "This is going to sound really strange, but believe me, there's an excellent reason for my question." She cleared her throat and plunged ahead. "Did you live in Chicago during the late seventies?"

"Who is this?"

"I don't know any cushy way to say this, so I'm going to spit it out. I'm Cynthia, your daughter. Cynthia Marie Williams."

"I don't know what you're talking about. You've got the wrong number."

"If your maiden name was Williams and you lived in Chicago for a while during the seventies, then yes, you do. You know exactly what I'm talking about."

"My God!" The hard thump of the receiver hitting the floor was followed by a startled gasp. Fumbling came next and finally Latonya spoke into the telephone. "I'm sorry. I dropped the telephone."

"That's okay."

"Who is this?" she demanded. "This isn't a game, a hoax, is it?"

"No. This is far too important to me. I'm Cynthia. Cynthia Williams, your daughter."

Another long pause followed and then a question, "How did you find me? I need some proof."

"Through a private investigator. The only proof I have is my birth certificate and the information I've always had about how you left me. I was seven months old when you left me with the state of Illinois welfare office. They sent me to their foster care division and I finally landed in a home."

The words rushed out as the tears fell, smearing the ink on Jacob's report in her hands. Cynthia didn't care. She was fighting for her future. The words needed to be said. It was imperative that she convince her mother of her identity.

"They moved me around for a couple of years until a couple named the Grants became my foster parents and they decided to keep me until I turned eighteen. My birth date is May 23, 1977. And I want to meet you. Talk to you about my life and find out about yours. Please?" Cynthia asked.

A muffled male voice came through the telephone line. "What's going on?"

"Who is it?" A young girl's voice carried through the phone line.

Cynthia tried again, dragging her mother's attention back to her. "Please."

"I-I-I," stammered the other woman.

"Please," she begged. "I need to talk with you."

An unbearable silence followed, but Cynthia held on, praying her mother would grant her request. There was a shift in Latonya's telephone demeanor. Cynthia felt as if Latonya had made a decision and now was in the process of executing a plan.

"All right," Latonya surrendered in a resigned voice. "When?"

"I'm here now," Cynthia explained, loosening her death grip on the telephone. "I mean in Detroit. My train got in about an hour ago and I'm staying at the Hyatt in Dearborn. Would you like to come here?"

"No, no. How long do you plan to stay in town?"

"Just a few days."

"I'm off tomorrow. Why don't you come here? Make it around three. Did you get a rental car? Or a way to get here?"

"No car. But, I can arrange for a driver to pick me up."

"Okay then. You have my telephone number, so I can assume you also have my address, correct?" A slight negative edge accompanied her words.

"Yes. But let me check. Is it 19538 West Outer Drive?"

"Correct. Come around three."

"Okay. And thank you."

"Mmm."

Quivering, Cynthia hung up. She took deep breaths, struggling to get her riotous pulse under control. Begging her mother for a visit was not the way she had wanted or expected this relationship to start. But she refused to allow her parent to dismiss her without providing some answers, clearing up some of her questions, and explaining what happened.

Her belly lunged and Cynthia sprang to her feet and rushed to the bathroom, hoping to make it to the toilet before she lost the White Castle hamburgers she had consumed on the train. After emptying her stomach, she sank to the floor, resting her head against the side of the cool porcelain bathtub.

She stayed that way for several moments before rising, rinsing her mouth, and brushing her teeth. Leaving the bathroom, she moved across the carpeted floor. There was one other thing she wanted to do before she rested.

Cynthia picked up the telephone and dialed David's hotel room. Regardless of their problems, she wanted to share this special moment with him. After several rings his voice mail kicked in and she hung up without leaving a message. She'd give him a try later.

I did it, Cynthia thought, giving herself a mental pat on the back. She returned to the bed as her remaining energy ebbed. Tired but content, she lay against the pillows. Waiting was going to be the worst part of this trip. The remainder of the day and night stretched before her.

As she lay there hugging a pillow, her thoughts returned to her mother. Her heart swelled with anticipation and fear in equal parts. After nearly twenty-six years, she believed she was prepared to meet her mother in less than twenty-four hours. Finally, she would have a family of her own.

Chapter 27

"Thank you." Cynthia stuffed the money through the plastic slot and glanced around her.

Asabi, her driver, removed the bills and counted them, placing her change in the same slot before asking, "Have you decided how you will get back to the hotel? I can return for you if necessary."

"Thank you." The tip of her tongue settled in the corner of her mouth as she considered his request. "But I'm not sure how long I'll actually be here. Umm, I've got your number." She patted the purse at her side. "I can call you when I'm ready to leave. Will that be okay?

"I'll be waiting." He tipped his head at her and a silent moment of empathy passed between them. "May this be the perfect day you seek and you receive many blessings."

"I hope so." Cynthia climbed out of the cab.

She stood on the curb, watching the cab disappear until all she saw was an orange dot. Asabi's words, "enjoy your day," returned to her. She sure hoped that happened. Last night Cynthia had paced the floor of the hotel room until the early hours of the morning, praying that everything would work out. After the night she spent in the hotel, she felt unsure of what the gods had in store for her.

Now, standing in front of Latonya Mason's home, she felt her emotions swinging from cold to hot. Her stomach performed somersaults, threatening to upchuck the dry toast and orange juice she'd forced down before leaving the hotel.

With each step closer to the house, her pulse increased dramatically and moisture dotted her forehead. *I'm terrified,* she thought, looking down at her trembling hands. What if they didn't like her? What would she do? She wished she'd listened to Lisa and let her tag along. Now would be a good time to have the support of her best friend.

A surge of longing swept through her as thoughts of David filled her head. Why couldn't he be here, at her side, offering words of encouragement and love?

David's not here. Once he learns that there won't be a baby, he'll probably skip out of my life, Cynthia silently chastised herself as she stood on the edge of the walkway. She held back for one additional beat, pulling her scattered emotions together.

Dressed in a caramel silk ankle-length Donna Karan dress with coordinating pumps, Cynthia wanted to portray an air of sophistication and composure, which was far from what she felt.

She took the first tentative step up the walkway and halted, examining her mother's home. A touch of pride filled her as she admired her residence. It felt good to know that Latonya Mason had made a decent life for herself.

It was a nice house, a very nice house. A three-car garage accompanied the beautiful redbrick colonial home on Bretton Drive. The large bay windows covered the front of the house. Cynthia could make out the outline of a black baby grand piano. The manicured lawn stretched green and healthy around a circular drive. Rows of colorful flowers welcomed visitors and accentuated the landscape. The house and its grounds were lovely.

At the heavy oak wine-red-stained door, she closed her eyes and took air deep into her lungs, praying that the day would be a major break-through. *I'm strong. I can do this,* Cynthia chanted silently to herself.

It took all of her energy to punch the doorbell and wait as patiently as humanly possible for some-one to answer. After several seconds that stretched like days, the door opened.

A petite woman stood on the opposite side of the door. She was dressed in a two-piece fuchsia capri pantsuit and black patent leather mules. The forty-odd-year-old woman wore dangling onyx jewelry partially hidden by her auburn hair, which was the same colors as Cynthia's. Silently, the two women examined each other.

Cynthia stared into a pair of almond-shaped clay-brown eyes that reflected guarded apprehension. She felt as if Latonya's gaze were searing her very soul. A stubborn chin jutted out at her. Cynthia got the distinct impression that Latonya Mason was not a person you messed with.

A silly grin formed on her lips and a warm glow

flowed through her. "Latonya Mason?" she asked quietly, holding her breath as she waited.

Hands clenched at her side, the woman answered tersely, "Yes."

"Good afternoon, I'm Cynthia."

Nodding, Latonya smiled smoothly, betraying nothing of her true feelings. She unhooked the storm door, opened it, then stepped back, allowing Cynthia to enter the foyer. "Come in."

Cynthia couldn't take her eyes off her mother; soft and round, Latonya was beautiful. The urge to touch her mother, or hug her, overwhelmed Cynthia. The flash of caution in Latonya's eyes halted her.

"We're in the great room." She shut and locked the door and started down a hallway.

Cynthia's heart took another leap. What did she mean we? Cynthia wondered, trailing her mother through the foyer. Could it be her father?

The walls of the foyer were beautifully painted in a marbleized faux finish. She stopped, studying a photo galley of five faces, each similar to her own. Delighted, Cynthia realized, *She had brothers and sisters!*

Silently, Latonya waited at the double-door entry of the living room. The cautious expression on her face squashed Cynthia's urge to ask a zillion questions.

A tall statuesque man waited silently near the piano with the shadow of the blinds obscuring his features. He turned as a familiar floral fragrance teased his nostrils.

"David!" she exclaimed, wanting to throw herself

in his arms. Her heart did a leap of joy at his solid and very welcome presence. He was elegantly dressed in a charcoal-gray suit with a tailored white shirt with French cuffs and a deep purple tie.

Hurrying across the hardwood floor, he gathered her into his arms. His soft lips touched her forehead. "Hey, hey, now," he whispered for her ears alone.

"You're here!" She hugged him close. "How did you find me?"

"You needed me. So I'm here. We'll talk about the rest later," David promised.

"Thank you."

"No problem. This is where I belong."

For the first time, Cynthia noticed a man sitting in a recliner in a corner of the room. Immediately, she recognized him from the photographs lining the foyer. Latonya perched on the edge of the recliner and laid a hand on the man's arm. "This is my husband, Gerald."

A million different emotions and questions besieged her. Was Gerald her father?

"Oh," Cynthia began, threading her fingers through David's. "I guess you already know this is my fiancé, David."

"Gerald is your father," Latonya stated in a voice that explained everything and nothing.

They're married! Cynthia's mind shouted as her heart thumped wildly in her chest.

Latonya's statement created a new series of questions. She studied this man who now had a place in her life. He looked so ordinary. But to her he meant so much more. Gerald represented a link to the past and to a part of her life that until today was empty. Hopefully, that link would include their future.

Her father rose from the chair, slim, but well over six feet in stature. As Gerald crossed the room his cocoa-brown face reflected hints of copper in the sunlight. He was casually dressed in a cream polo golf shirt, olive Dockers, and Cole Haan loafers.

She'd misjudged his physical appearance. There was nothing ordinary about him. He was a striking man. Gerald stopped in front of her, showing no emotion as he gazed into her upturned face.

Cynthia waited, expecting to feel the warmth of an emotional link between herself and her father. She shivered as the cool silence permeated the air. *This does not feel right.* She reached for her earlobe, caressing her lucky pearl earring for comfort. Had she said or done something wrong? Where was the love?

Goose bumps formed on the surface of her skin as he studied her. He bowed his head a bit and offered her a stiff smile that revealed a tiny gap between his front teeth.

She giggled behind her hand, attempting to stifle her nervous reaction.

Waving a hand at the sofa, he said in a melodious baritone voice, "Why don't you have a seat? Get comfortable so that we can talk."

As they complied, an awkward silence settled over the small group as they waited for someone to break the ice. Cynthia clung to David's hand, needing his support. Latonya drew in an impatient breath, expelled it, and rubbed at the chair's sage-green raw silk fabric. "Well, I'm sure you have questions. So let's hear them. Ask away."

Cynthia stammered, "Wh-wh-what happened?"

"I don't know what you know about me. Us. I was young and living away from home for the first time. It was my freshman year of college. I started out at the University of Chicago. It's a pretty common story. I got pregnant and tried to stay in school and keep you." Somewhat embarrassed, she glanced away. "It didn't work. I couldn't handle it."

Cynthia focused on the silent man at her side. "What about G-G-Gerald? Didn't he help?"

"I stayed here," her father explained. "Struggling to keep my business from crashing."

Up to this point, David had been silent, allowing Cynthia to quiz her parents. "What is your profession, Mr. Mason?"

"I own a cooling and heating business."

"Mmm," David muttered.

"Your mother and I hung together in high school. My family had Mason's Cooling and Heating and I was next in line to take over. Toya wanted to go to college and got accepted to the University of Chicago. We stayed tight even though it was a long-distance relationship. Sometimes on the weekend, I'd drive to see her."

An unplanned pregnancy was pretty much what Cynthia expected. But finding them together amazed her. Leaning forward, she fired a series of questions. "The agency told me that you left me and never came back." It hurt to say those words. "Did you return to Detroit? Why didn't you bring me with you? Where was Gerald? Did you ever try to find me?"

"Cyn," David warned in a soft tone, squeezing her hand. "Give her a minute to answer."

"When I got home there was so much going on in my family. My mother had had a stroke and needed constant care. My father couldn't cope so he didn't help and the burden of all of that was left for me. I couldn't handle a baby along with everything else. I felt that I had made the correct decision in leaving you with people who could look out for you."

"Did you ever look for me? Ask for any records about me?" Her voice rose an octave with each question.

Latonya's gaze became fixed on a painting beyond Cynthia's shoulder. "My mother died that summer and my father followed her six weeks later. I didn't have time to think."

"What about Chicago?" Cynthia pushed on. Her euphoria was rapidly fading into something unpleasant. "Did you ever return?"

"No. I finished my degree here in Detroit at Wayne State University."

Sensing Cynthia's frustration, David took charge. "Mrs. Mason, Cynthia and I decided to search for you for a very specific reason. We are going to have a baby. One of our concerns involves your medical history. Could you give us a little information? You said your mother had a stroke. Did she also suffer with high blood pressure?"

She nodded, relaxing now that she was on more familiar territory. "Yes. I have it, as well. But it's all under control. My mother never complied; she ate wrong and never took her medicine correctly."

David continued, "Was there anything else that we should be concerned with? Any diabetes, lupus, or cancer in your family?"

"No."

"I noticed the photographs in the hallway." David pointed in that direction. "Those are your children, correct?"

"Yes," Gerald answered.

"Any health issues with your kids?"

"No," Latonya sighed, tightening her grip on her chair. "I hope we've given you the answers you need," she offered with a hesitant smile.

Cynthia lifted a hand. "I have a question. I have siblings? Correct?"

"Yes," Gerald chimed in.

"Don't you think we should meet?" Cynthia asked.

Latonya straightened her posture on the arm of the chair. She turned to her husband and cleared her throat before saying, "Gerald and I discussed this last night. You have your own life in Chicago." She waved a hand in David's direction. "Soon you'll have a family of your own and a new husband. We think it would be best to keep our kids out of this. They don't know anything about you. There would be so many questions and we don't want to disrupt their lives."

Fighting back tears, Cynthia understood then that they didn't want her. She willed the anguish flooding her soul not to spill from her eyes. Latonya and Gerald Mason lived the life that they enjoyed, and her arriving on their doorstep presented a complication that they didn't want.

"I hope this explained everything for you so that you can go back to Chicago with your questions answered," Gerald stated.

His statement was delivered in an emotionless voice that chilled her. She felt as if a hand had closed around her heart and squeezed the life from it.

Questions answered. Was that all they had to say? The family reconciliation she wished for had become a distant dream. There were no words of encouragement, invitations to return to Detroit. They had cooperated and now they wanted her to leave.

Cynthia stared at her mother, speechless. "What about my life?" she asked. "How about what I've gone through?"

Gerald cleared her throat. "We could never have been the parents you deserved at that time. But things worked out for you."

Latonya chimed in encouragingly. "You're doing well. David told us about your job at Games People Play and how you won a scholarship, got your master's degree. That's wonderful. We're happy for you and we wish you much success."

There was her kiss-off.

Latonya continued in a conciliatory tone, "Our children are not at home because we've raised them with certain beliefs and we don't want to change that."

Translation, you were our big mistake and we don't want our children to know about you. Cynthia tried to force her confused emotions into some order, but nothing made any sense.

Frowning, she tugged her hand away from David and stared at her parents. "Don't you want to know about me? Who I am? What's happened in my life?"

"You look well," Latonya reasoned, looking past her. "A handsome young man followed you here, so that tells me that you have someone who cares about you."

"I see," Cynthia snapped.

David rose from his place on the sofa, helped her to her feet, and started across the room. "Thank you for your time. We appreciate it."

Cynthia resisted, certain she was missing something. There had to be more she could do to bring her family together. This was what she dreamed of all her life and it was all falling apart.

David tugged on her hand and she followed.

Latonya and Gerald followed them to the door in silence. Cynthia's heart was breaking. *How could they not want to know about her.* She wondered. Wasn't she a part of them?

She just didn't matter. The Masons were content with their family and she wasn't part of it. This was more painful than not knowing about them.

Pride kept her tears at bay until they were out of the house and standing on the porch. The door closed behind them and Cynthia reached for David, needing him more than she ever had. He wrapped her in his arms and held her close, uttering words of love. And for the first time since childhood, she gave in to her tears in public. Deep sobs racked her as all of her pain and frustration manifested through her tears. Through it all David held her, offering solace and comfort, until she was done.

Chapter 28

David helped Cynthia from the car. He wrapped a firm arm around her shoulders and hurried through the Hyatt's lobby. Their elevator ride was completed in a tense, unhappy silence and his concern escalated a notch.

Wrapped in a silken cocoon of pain, Cynthia remained withdrawn and oblivious to her surroundings. Her eyes were red-rimmed and tears still lingered on her dark eyelashes. She hadn't said a word since they left her parents' home, and David was worried, deeply troubled about her mental state. He took a second to study the layout of the room. As hotel accommodations went, this one was ordinary and easily dismissed. He led her away from the door and pushed her into one of the cream-and-white-striped chairs.

David ran his hand over his hair, searching for a way to pull her out of her blue funk. His eyes swept the room and settled on a black pint-sized coffeemaker perched on top of a brown portable refrigerator. Focusing all of his energy on Cynthia, he asked in a cheery, persuasive tone, "How about a cup of tea?"

No response followed.

Stripping off his suit jacket, David dropped it on the bed, rolled back his shirtsleeves, and went to work. Five minutes later, he wrapped Cynthia's cold, lifeless hands around a yellow mug of steaming cinnamon apple tea. "Come on, sweetheart. Drink up. It'll put some color in your cheeks."

Raw hurt was quickly replaced by bewilderment. Cynthia studied the mug in her hands in a way that suggested she couldn't figure out how she got it. On his knees at her side, David took advantage of her confusion by placing a hand under the mug and lifting it to her lips.

After a moment, she sipped the brew. His mouth curved into an approving smile; she was coming out of the funk. His smile disappeared as he realized that nothing would erase the pain of how her family had treated her. In the past, talking about a problem always made Cyn feel better.

"I guess you were right," she stated in a voice heavy with pain and regret. "They don't want me."

Shocked, David whipped around and stared at her for a long moment. The expression on her face hurt him. He'd do anything to make it vanish.

Cynthia needed him to offer the right encouragement. He rubbed a palm down his cheek, choosing his words very carefully. Returning to the spot next to her chair, he cradled her hand between both of his, brought it to his mouth, and kissed her palm. "No, they didn't. I didn't want to be correct about them." Those were hard words to say, but anything less would have been a lie and Cynthia deserved the truth.

"I know," she whispered. Her lips quivered as she fought for control.

He reached inside his trouser pocket, produced a handkerchief, and handed it to her. Cynthia mopped away her tears, then twisted the silk around her fingers. "And now you know that," he said.

She nodded her head in dismay.

"Sweetheart, it's time to let them go." Cynthia tugged at her hand, but he refused to release it. "I know you had great expectations for today. And you prayed for a completely different outcome. I know you can't see it, but the day was still a success."

"Success?" Her eyes narrowed and he knew she was going to tear him apart.

"Hold on. Let me explain."

Her mouth snapped shut and she waited.

"Part of what you wanted did come true. You met the people who gave you life. Plus, you found out that you have siblings. Family."

"Yeah. My parents don't want me to get to know them."

"That doesn't matter," he dismissed with a wave of his hand. "One day they'll be adults just like you and you can contact them and invite them into your life. It may not happen today, but it can happen in your future. Have a little faith."

He stood and held out his hand. Cynthia placed hers in his palm and he led her to the bed. They sat on the edge, fingers linked together. David stretched his long legs in front of him.

"Cyn, don't take on your parents' issues," he

warned. "It isn't you; it's them. If they don't see the wonderful person they created, shame on them."

"Oh, David," she began, brushing her hair away from her face. "I wanted to be part of their family so much. I dreamed of having people who looked like me be in my life."

"Genes are only a part of what makes up a family," he reminded her, cupping her cheek. "I don't think your family has to look exactly like you. I believe it involves much more. Like commitment, connection." He whispered the next word with all the emotion he felt for her. "Love. Those things make a family and help people bond. Did you feel any of those emotions with your mother or father?"

The room was silent as she considered his question. "No," she answered, shaking her head. "I have more of a connection with Miss Helen and Mr. Nick."

"Why?" he asked. Gathering her into his arms, he held her closely against the length of his body, allowing his warmth to penetrate the thin fabric of her dress.

"I don't know." She shrugged, then stopped as her forehead wrinkled. "Because they've always been part of my life. When I got in trouble, they fought for me and stood by me when I needed them. I never worried that they would be at my side because they were always right there, helping, supporting, loving me."

"Exactly!" he yelped, pointing a finger at her. "You have a family. You always have. All you need to do is admit it and accept them."

Cynthia untangled herself from David's arms,

rose from the bed, and stepped into the bathroom. She needed a few minutes to clear her head. Raking her hands through her hair, she turned on the faucet and ran water into the deep beige sink as she studied her face in the mirror.

Woo, I look a mess, she thought. Her eyes were red and puffy. Mascara stained her cheeks and all traces of her lipstick were missing. A cold shiver spread over her as she remembered all that had happened. The day had certainly taken its toll on her. She collected a white fluffy towel and matching washcloth from the rack above the toilet and began to repair the damage made by the emotional roller coaster she'd been on all day. With her looking like this, David should have run screaming from the room. *Oh, David,* she thought, remembering how he'd held her during her torrent of tears. She didn't know what she would have done today without David. He'd been her anchor.

Once she repaired her makeup, she gathered her courage and returned to the room, searching for him. David had abandoned the bed and was now sitting in one of the chairs, watching the news with a glass of orange juice in his hand.

His dark brown eyes softened at the sight of her. "You look better."

"Thanks." She smiled shyly. "I feel better because of you."

With a gallant dip of his head, he stated, "Think nothing of it."

Cynthia dropped onto the bed, wanting to put all the pieces together. "You know, everything has been so crazy I forgot to ask, what are you doing here? I mean, I appreciate it, I really do. I needed you." Restless, she stroked the tan, blue, and cream comforter. "But, according to Autumn Snyder, you were knee-deep in Dytech depositions."

"Yeah, I was."

"Was?" Cynthia wondered.

"When we get back to Chicago, you may have an unemployed fiancé."

She was too startled by his statement to offer any comment.

He grabbed the remote and turned off the television, giving her his full attention. "I wanted to be here with you. So I came."

Studying him under lowered lashes, she asked, "You left the case without finishing the work?"

His nodded. "More or less."

"David, what were you thinking?" She rose from the bed and met him in the center of the room.

"Sweetheart, I made enough mistakes. I wasn't going to make any more. I was thinking that you needed me and that you are the most important thing in my life." As he stroked her cheek, David's eyes brimmed with tenderness and love. "So I had to get to you. Be here for you. I did the right thing."

"You put your future in jeopardy."

He swallowed the last of his juice and placed the empty glass on the nightstand. "Maybe I did. I won't know until I get back to Chicago. I'm done with Ruffino's threats."

"Threats? What kind of threats?"

He sighed and his hand dropped to his side. "I didn't want to talk about this now. I was hoping we could ease into it later."

She nudged him with her elbow. "Tell me."

"The day before we were supposed to get married, I went by the office to make sure my team had everything under control. On my way out, I ran into Ruffino."

At the mention of their put-off wedding, her pulse quickened. Maybe she wasn't ready to hear this.

"Let's just say, Ruffino made me an offer I was afraid to refuse." Hands clenched into fists, David uttered the name like a dirty word.

She frowned. "Oh, David. What have you done?"

"I made a decision and I don't regret it. I don't know if I've ever told you this and I'm not sure you were around our house at the time, but when I was growing up, it was very rough for my parents financially. We had the things we needed, like clothes, food, and a home. But Mom and Dad were on a tight budget most of my childhood."

That explained a lot about David. Things she had never understood. Why he felt he had to excel at everything he tried. His desire to give her everything. It made perfect sense. He didn't want his family to suffer in any way.

"Don't get me wrong. I love my folks and I know they did their best. I wanted more. And I wanted to give you more." David shut his eyes, reliving those difficult times. "I hated that we were so strapped. I promised myself that my family would never live that way. And that's how Ruffino had me, because I wanted you to be free of money worries."

"Money is not that important to me. I told you before I needed a partner, not a breadwinner. I can take care of myself."

"Yeah, you did."

"Would you go back to Ruffino, Hartman and Black if the opportunity presented itself?" she asked hesitantly.

"No." He shook his head, shoving his hands into the pockets of his trousers. "I need something different. I've been thinking about either opening my own practice or working in the district attorney's office."

Surprise narrowed her brown eyes. "That'll be a big change. Are you sure it's what you want?"

"After Dytech, I need to feel as if I'm making a difference. I want to fight for the rights of Chicago residents. I believe that's where I belong now."

"What happened with Dytech?"

"They're guilty. And they're going to get away with it," he muttered between clenched teeth. "It bugs me that they stole from retirees. And if I go back, I'll have to defend them. I can't do that."

"I'll support you in whatever you decide to do," Cynthia promised earnestly.

"Good." He drew her into his arms, laughing into her hair. "Because you might be the breadwinner if I'm out of a job."

Chapter 29

Sweet Georgia Brown was located in downtown Detroit. Tastefully decorated in soft, muted tones of green, brown, and ivory; the restaurant displayed an understated elegance.

Cynthia wasn't sure they were doing the right thing in coming here. They had a lot to discuss and maybe a restaurant was the wrong venue to air their dirty laundry. But they needed to eat and since their plane didn't leave until later that evening, they decided to enjoy some of the local cuisine.

They were seated at a round table covered by a white linen tablecloth. A gentleman attired in a jacket and black trousers approached. "Good evening." He bowed slightly from the waist. "I'm Eugene. And I'll be your server tonight. Can I start you off with a cocktail?"

He removed the linen napkins from the water glasses, draping them across Cynthia's and then David's laps, and hurried off to bar. Eugene returned with their drinks and took two orders of Sweet Georgia Brown's trio combination of fried lobster, crab cake, and shrimp with asparagus in hollandaise sauce and red potatoes.

They concentrated on their meal, leaving conversation for later. When she was finished, Cynthia leaned back in her chair and sighed dreamily. "That was heavenly."

Sipping on a glass of lemonade, David nodded. "It certainly was."

He watched her for a silent moment, then asked in a husky rumble, "Sweetheart, there's something on your mind, isn't there? Want to share?"

Panic rose inside her. She glanced at him, then turned away, pleating the edge of the tablecloth. She had hoped to have dessert before she told this particular secret. "There is," she admitted. "But I'm nervous about telling you."

"There's no reason for you to be nervous." He smiled encouragingly, taking her by the hand. "You can tell me anything."

She felt as if he could see into her soul at that moment. There wasn't an easy way to tell him, so she just spit it out. "I'm not pregnant."

His head snapped back as if she'd slapped him across the face and his eyes narrowed. "What?"

"We're not going to have a baby. I found out while you were in Philadelphia."

"But, I . . . um." Massaging his forehead, he said, "Go on."

"Dr. Noah did some blood work and located a small cyst on my ovary." She drew in a fortifying breath. "That's what was causing my problem."

"Man," he muttered, leaning his head against the back of the chair. He sat up. His gaze ran over her body, examining her with a critical eye. "Are you all right?"

She'd lost a baby that never existed, but it had been real to her. She wasn't great, but she was doing better. "Don't worry. I'm fine. How do you feel about this?"

A look of tired sadness passed over his features. "Disappointed. I was looking forward to our baby, to raising him together and being a family. I wanted that."

"Me too." Heaviness centered in her chest. "I'm sorry."

Cynthia felt his touch on her arm.

"It's not your fault."

"In some way I think it's a good thing that I'm not pregnant."

"Why would you say that?" He stared at her as if he'd never seen her before. "I mean, it's been a rough time for us, yes. But I always believed that we would get through it together."

"I don't think we were ready for marriage."

David looked shocked. "Of course we were. We were getting married."

"That didn't matter."

A knowing expression flashed across his face and he nodded. "You're not doing this because I stood you up, are you?"

"No. Although I have to admit you leaving town gave me time to rethink my life. I don't want to get married because I have to. When I walk down the aisle, I want to do it because it's the right thing for me."

"Are you saying you don't love me?"

"I've loved you since the seventh grade and I still love you," she answered in a sure tone. "Pregnancy made marriage an urgent issue. I don't want to do that. I want you to marry me because you can't imagine your life without me in it, not because a baby needs a father."

"What do you want to do? Break up?" His voice was full of uncertainty. Cynthia thought she heard it crack. "Go our separate ways? Because I can tell you right now that I'm not going to lose you. I love you too much."

"And I love you," she responded immediately. "I'm suggesting that we have a cooling-down period, nonengagement time where we can get to know each other again." Cynthia waved her hands back and forth between them, searching for the correct word. "Reconnect. Let's go home and date."

"Then what?"

"Then you can ask me to marry you again."

Epilogue

One year later

Cynthia watched the activity around her. She had everything she ever wanted. The man she loved, a family, and now marriage.

The soft strings of violins reached Cynthia's nervous ears. The front door repeatedly opened and closed as the guests arrived. This was the day she dreamed of. A wedding where everyone she loved was present. She sat patiently, waiting for Mom to put the final touches to her bridal outfit.

David had been right. She had a family. A family that loved and supported her.

"These were my grandmother's." Mom extended a string of pearls before Cynthia. "They've been in my family for years and I want you to wear them for good luck. Now you have something borrowed."

Touched by this gesture, Cynthia admired the necklace. They fit so perfectly with the beaded bodice of her ivory gown. "Oh, Mom. They're gorgeous." She gave David's mother a tight hug. "Thank you."

"Let me take a look at you. Your wedding dress is

new. The pearls will work double duty as something old and borrowed. What about blue? What do you have that's blue?"

"I've got it." Vee waved a blue lace handkerchief in the air. "Cyn, I'd like you to have this."

"It's beautiful. Thank you." Touched by Vee's thoughtfulness, Cynthia took the lace fabric, fingering the intricate embroidery along the edge of the cloth. When she opened the hankie, she saw her initials embroidered in gold.

"I added your initials myself," Vee announced proudly. "I wanted you to have something special from me." She brushed a handful of braided hair over her shoulder and grinned. "This is so cool. Now I have three sisters."

A soft tap on the door startled everyone. "Ladies, it's time to get this show on the road," Dad's happy voice boomed.

"He's right. So let's get going." Mom stepped forward and took charge. "Lisa, Cynthia, you wait while I get Vee and Jenn situated."

Lisa moved to Cynthia's side and took her hand, squeezing it. Cynthia glanced at their linked fingers, stroking Lisa's wedding ring. "I only hope that we are as happy as you and Matthew."

With tears in her eyes, Lisa answered, "I couldn't wish for anything better for you. Cynthia, be happy. Love each other and the rest will come."

Mom reentered the room. "Cynthia, Lisa. It's your turn."

Dad was waiting at the door for them. He took Cynthia's arm and led her down the stairs to the living room. The wedding march began to play. "This is our song," he stated with pride. They moved down the center of the room.

The living room was filled with flowers, guests, and love. Everything was perfect.

As they made their way to David, she couldn't help feeling as if she'd hit the jackpot, won the major prize that she'd always dreamed of.

Dressed in a dove-gray tux, David looked handsome and confident. J.D. and Eddie were at his side. When she reached him, he took her hand and brought it to his lips, kissing her palm. Cynthia felt as if he were the most precious gift in the world.

She mouthed the words. "I love you."

"I love you more," he whispered to her. They turned to the judge who would join their lives forever.

ABOUT THE AUTHOR

Karen White-Owens was born in Detroit, Michigan and resides in the Motor City. She holds a bachelor's degree in sociology from Wayne State University and is working toward a master's in library and information science.

In addition to writing, she manages an after-school program for a charter school in the Detroit area. She devotes her free time to editing manuscripts for aspiring authors. During the 1999–2000 and 2000–2001 school years she taught the fundamentals of creative writing to the students of the Detroit Writers Guild Young Authors Program (YAP).

Currently, she works as a part-time instructor at Wayne State University's Interdisciplinary Studies Program, teaching writing communication skills to undergraduate students. As a devoted supporter of the Detroit Writers Guild Annual Conferences, she has conducted workshops on characterization and rejection letters and has provided manuscript critiquping.

Gary, her husband of thirteen years, is her biggest fan.

BOOK YOUR PLACE ON OUR WEBSITE AND MAKE THE ARABESQUE ROMANCE CONNECTION!

We've created a customized website just for our very special Arabesque readers, where you can get the inside scoop on everything that's going on with Arabesque romance novels.

When you come online, you'll have the exciting opportunity to:

- View covers of upcoming books

- Learn about our future publishing schedule (listed by publication month and author)

- Find out when your favorite authors will be visiting a city near you

- Search for and order backlist books

- Check out author bios and background information

- Send e-mail to your favorite authors

- Join us in weekly chats with authors, readers and other guests

- Get writing guidelines

- AND MUCH MORE!

Visit our website at
http://www.arabesquebooks.com